BEFORE HE HARMS

BEFORE HE HARMS

(A Mackenzie White Mystery—Book 14)

BLAKE PIERCE

BLAKE PIERCE

Blake Pierce is the USA Today bestselling author of the RILEY PAGE mystery series, which includes seventeen books. Blake Pierce is also the author of the MACKENZIE WHITE mystery series, comprising fourteen books; of the AVERY BLACK mystery series, comprising six books; of the KERI LOCKE mystery series, comprising five books; of the MAKING OF RILEY PAIGE mystery series, comprising six books; of the KATE WISE mystery series, comprising seven books; of the CHLOE FINE psychological suspense mystery, comprising six books; of the JESSE HUNT psychological suspense thriller series, comprising seven books (and counting); of the AU PAIR psychological suspense thriller series, comprising two books (and counting); of the ZOE PRIME mystery series, comprising three books (and counting); of the new ADELE SHARP mystery series; and of the new EUROPEAN VOYAGE cozy mystery series.

ONCE GONE (a Riley Paige Mystery—Book #1), BEFORE HE KILLS (A Mackenzie White Mystery—Book I), CAUSE TO KILL (An Avery Black Mystery—Book I), A TRACE OF DEATH (A Keri Locke Mystery—Book I), WATCHING (The Making of Riley Paige—Book I), NEXT DOOR (A Chloe Fine Psychological Suspense Mystery—Book I), THE PERFECT WIFE (A Jessie Hunt Psychological Suspense Thriller—Book One), and IF SHE KNEW (A Kate Wise Mystery—Book I) are each available as a free download on Amazon!

An avid reader and lifelong fan of the mystery and thriller genres, Blake loves to hear from you, so please feel free to visit www.blakepierceauthor.com to learn more and stay in touch.

TABLE OF CONTENTS

CHAPTER ONE

She was nearly slipping with each step, her feet sliding in her open-toed sandals as she ran through the damp field. It was night now, and there were little wisps of mist covering the ground from where the afternoon's drizzle of rain had passed through. It didn't seem like much, but she couldn't help but wonder if that little bit of moisture in the bottom of her sandals was going to be responsible for her death.

They had found her. She had no idea how, but they had.

The only chance she had of getting through this night alive was getting to Amy. The way she figured it, she had about another two miles of running. If she could make it through this stupid wet field, Amy's neighborhood was two miles away.

Irritated with the slipping and sliding, she stopped long enough to take the sandals off. If she'd had more time to prepare, she would have put on her sneakers but it had all happened so fast...

She held the sandals in her right hand and continued to run. It was a bit easier, though her tender feet started to complain instantly about the hard earth beneath the grass. She looked past the pain and ran as hard as she could. She had to get to Amy.

She glanced back behind her and saw only the staggered shape of the forest—trees rising and falling in the darkness like some strange graph. If there was someone following her, she could not see them. She wasn't naïve enough to think they weren't on to her, though. Certainly someone was looking for her, making sure she told no one.

The field came to an abrupt stop and suddenly, she found herself leaping across a ditch and onto a two-lane road. When she landed on the road, she skidded a bit, the tar biting into her heels. She looked to her right and saw the glow of streetlights in the distance. Amy would be there, somewhere in the midst of all of that glowing. This knowledge had her legs pumping even though they were screaming in pain from the several miles she had already run through the forest and the fields to get here.

She ran down the road, figuring there was at least half a mile between her and those glowing lights. She thought of her cell phone, lost somewhere back in the forest, and thought of how easy it would be to just call. She could have cried at the frustration.

As she ran, she did allow herself to cry. She ran and wept and dug deep into her lungs for her next breath.

Somehow, she came to the neighborhood. Her legs felt like jelly and she was so out of breath that she saw little black fireworks in her field of vision. But that was okay, because she was here now. She'd get to Amy. Amy would know what to do. She wasn't sure if it was even worth trying to contact the police, but that might not matter. All she needed to do was to get in touch with Amy. The thought of it was a relief.

She nearly started calling Amy's name as she neared her house. Just four or five more houses down and she'd be safe. The streetlights were rather dim thanks to the mist from the recent rain and the entire neighborhood looked like something out of a horror movie, but Amy's house was up there somewhere like a lighthouse.

She was putting so much focus on the shape of the houses that she did not hear the purring engine behind her. When she finally heard the car, she looked over her shoulder. When she saw it screaming toward her with its headlights off, she tried dashing hard to the right, but it did little good.

The car struck her hard on the right side. Everything went numb for a moment as she did half a cartwheel three feet in the air. But the pain all came racing on in a fury when she struck the pavement. Her head rocked off of the road and the world went mostly black.

This was why she was unable to see the face of the figure that parked the car in the middle of the street, got out, and pulled a knife on her.

She knew the person was slitting her throat, but the pain in her head and back blissfully masked that one particular pain.

The life went rushing out of her as the killer walked back to their car.

He and the car were both gone as she took her last breath on the rain-slicked road.

Chapter Two

The apartment smelled like rosemary and lemon as dinner cooked on the stove, the first bottle of wine had been opened, and The Cure was playing on Spotify. To any random visitor, it might appear as if Mackenzie White was having a splendid afternoon. But what they would not see was the internal struggle and the anxiousness that had her nerves and stomach on edge.

The chicken was done and the asparagus was in the oven. Mackenzie sipped from a glass of red wine, trying to find something to do. Ellington was on the living room floor with Kevin, reading him a book. He looked up at her and rolled his eyes. When he came to an appropriate stopping point—where the Poky Little Puppy once again crawled under the fence—he hefted Kevin up in his arms and entered the kitchen.

"It's just your mother," he said. "You're acting like we're about to visited by the IRS or something."

"You've haven't met her," Mackenzie said.

"She anything like you?"

"Aside from the whole abandonment thing, yeah."

"Then I'm sure she's fine. You just tell me how much charm I need to lay on."

"Not too much. She won't get your jokes."

"I take it back then," Ellington said. "I hate the woman already." He kissed Kevin's forehead and shrugged. "She does have the right to meet her grandson, though. Aren't you at all glad she wants to be involved?"

"I want to be. But it's hard for me to trust her."

"I get that," Ellington said. "I don't exactly get the warm fuzzies when it come to my mom either."

"Yes, but at least she came knocking when you had a child, right?"

"That she did. But let's not assume that's a good thing. It might be years before we realize the traumatic impact that has on Kevin."

"I'm not joking here, E. The woman is toxic. She's just—"

She trailed off, not sure of how to end the comment. She's just *what?* Selfish would be a fitting word. Immature would be another. The woman had essentially closed herself off after her husband had been killed and, as such, Mackenzie and her sister had been left without much of a mother-figure at all.

"She's your mother," Ellington said. "And I'm excited to meet her."

"I'll remind you of those words about an hour into her visit."

They shared a kiss and Ellington returned to the living room to continue reading about the misadventures of the Poky Little Puppy. Mackenzie listened in as she sipped from her wine again and started to set the table. She glanced to the clock, noting that there were only six minutes left before her mother was set to show up. She had to admit, dinner smelled delicious and Kevin was looking more adorable than ever. He was getting too damned old for her liking. He was pulling himself up and scooting; they were fully expecting him to take his first steps any day now.

It was a good reminder of how long it had been since she'd seen her mother. Her son was about to walk now and her mother hadn't—

A knock on the door interrupted her thoughts. She gave Ellington a startled look, to which he grinned, picked Kevin back up, and extended his free hand toward her. He'd been free of the cast from his previous injuries for about a week now, and it was good to see him using both arms comfortably.

She took it and he pulled her to him. "You take down some of the roughest people our society has to offer," he reminded her. "Certainly you can make it through this."

She nodded, and they walked together to the door. When they answered it, Mackenzie had to take a moment to collect her thoughts.

Her mother looked beautiful. She had taken care of herself in the months that had passed since she'd last seen her; Mackenzie thought that might have been almost a year at this point but wasn't quite sure. She looked healthy and actually *happy.* Her hair was done nicely and she looked maybe ten years younger than her actual age of fifty-three.

"Hey, Mom," Mackenzie said. "You look nice."

"You do, too." She looked past Mackenzie and then to Ellington, holding Kevin. "Sorry," she said. "We haven't officially met."

Watching her mother and Ellington shake hands was beyond surreal. And when Mackenzie saw Kevin studying the strange woman at their doorstep, her heart broke a bit. She had given something of an open invitation to her mother a little less than a year ago when she had gone out to Nebraska to tell her she was a grandmother. And it had taken her *this* long to take her up on it. To her credit, though, she had declined Mackenzie's offer to pay for the plane fare.

"Come on in, Mom," Mackenzie said.

Patricia White stepped into her daughter's apartment as if she were entering some sort of cathedral—with reverence and respect. As soon as the door was closed behind her, she looked at Kevin and then, with tears in her eyes, back to Mackenzie.

"Can I hold him?"

"You're his grandmother," Mackenzie said. "Of course you can."

When Ellington handed Kevin over, he did so without any hesitation. He was watching his mother-in-law's expression of awe and gratitude with the same focus as Mackenzie. While Mackenzie was glad to see her mother holding Kevin, there was certainly something surreal about it all.

"He looks just like you," Patricia said to her daughter.

"A good thing," Ellington said with a chuckle.

Mackenzie led her mother deeper into her apartment, bringing her into the living room. They sat down together, Mackenzie and Ellington sharing a look over Patricia's head as they settled down. Ellington gave her an *I-told-you-so* look which she returned with a scowl.

"You didn't already check into a hotel, did you?" Mackenzie asked.

"I did. Already dropped my stuff off." She never took her eyes away from Kevin as she spoke. Mackenzie wasn't sure she had ever seen her mother smile so big in her life.

"You didn't have to do that, Mom. I told you that you're welcome to stay here."

"I know," she said, finally taking her eyes away from her grandson as she bounced him on her knee. "But you both have busy jobs and I didn't want to get in the way. Besides, I have a hot tub in my room for tonight and some sightseeing to do tomorrow. I've never been to DC before, so . . ."

She stopped here, as if that ended the entire conversation. And as far as Mackenzie was concerned, it did.

"Well, dinner is just about ready," Mackenzie said. "Another few minutes. The table is already set if we want to move in there."

They did just that, Patricia taking Kevin with her as Ellington moved Kevin's highchair to the edge of the dining table. As they all settled in, Ellington pouring wine for himself and Patricia, Mackenzie brought the dinner in bit by bit. She'd always had something of a knack for cooking, but she had to stick to simple things. Tonight's offering was a simple four-ingredient rosemary-lemon chicken with potatoes and asparagus. Patricia looked as it as if this, too, surprised her.

"You know how to cook?" she asked.

"Somewhat. I'm not great."

"She's being modest," Ellington said.

"She always was."

And just like that, dinner began. The conversation was a bit awkward, but not painful. Ellington spent most of the time talking, letting Patricia know more about him: where he was raised, how long he'd been an agent, and his version of how his relationship with her daughter had started. Mackenzie was also surprised at how much it meant to her when her mother complimented her cooking. The entire time, Kevin sat in his highchair, eating little bits of chicken that Mackenzie cut off for him. He was getting quite good at feeding himself with his hands, but a good amount of food still ended up on the floor.

By the time everyone's plate had been cleaned and the bottle of wine was empty, Mackenzie realized that there was a very good chance this was not going to be the train wreck she had feared. With dinner over, Ellington tidied up Kevin and gave him a few yogurt melts before clearing off the table. Mackenzie sat across from her mother while the sounds of Ellington filling the dishwasher came from the kitchen.

"I don't suppose you've spoken with your sister lately?" Patricia said.

"No. The last time we spoke, you said she was in LA, right?"

"Yes. And if that's changed, she hasn't reached out to speak with me. I swear, it seems like she just became even more distant once you wrapped the case concerning your father. I never understood how she—"

She was interrupted by a knock at the apartment door... which was curious, because it was rare that she and Ellington ever got visitors.

"Babe, can you get that?" Ellington called from the kitchen. "I'm elbow-deep in dirty dishes."

"One second, Mom," Mackenzie said, getting up from the table. She gave Kevin a playful little tweak on the nose as she passed by. She was surprised at how well this was going. She might even dare say she was enjoying the visit. The afternoon was going remarkably well.

She answered the door with a slight spring her step. Yet, when she answered it, the spring snapped and the real world came roaring back toward her.

"Hello, Mackenzie," said the woman at the door.

Mackenzie tried on a fake smile that didn't quite fit. "Hey, E," she called out over her shoulder. "Your mom is here."

CHAPTER THREE

Mackenzie honestly had nothing against Frances Ellington. She'd been something of a saving grace when Mackenzie had gone back to work, stepping in and watching Kevin for them. It also didn't hurt that Kevin loved his Grandma E very much. But the idea of having both grandmothers in the same place at the same time was incredibly unsettling. Mackenzie felt she knew both women well enough to know that it was the equivalent of pushing a powder keg down a hill where a raging fire was growing.

Slowly, timidly, Mackenzie led Frances into the dining room. The moment Kevin saw her, his face lit up and he held his arms out. Behind them, Ellington came into the room with a dumbfounded look on his face.

"Mom . . . what are you doing here?"

"I was in the neighborhood and thought I'd stop by to take you guys out to dinner, but it looks like I was a little late."

"You would have known that if you'd called."

Frances ignored her son, spotted Patricia sitting at the table, and flashed a huge smile. "I'm Frances Ellington, by the way."

"And I'm Patricia White," Patricia said. "It's good to meet you."

There was an incredibly tense silence that everyone could feel. It seemed even Kevin was taken aback, looking around the room to see if something was wrong. His eyes finally landed on Mackenzie and when she gave him a big smile, that seemed to be the end of it for him.

"Well, if we're all going to be here, I may as well break out dessert," Ellington said. "It's not much, just an ice cream cake that was calling my name at the grocery store yesterday."

"It sounds lovely," Frances said as she sat down in the chair next to Kevin. Kevin gave her his undivided attention, his new grandmother now totally forgotten.

"Frances watches him from time to time," Mackenzie explained to her mother. She hoped that simple statement was mindful because to Mackenzie's ear, it sounded almost like an accusation. *She keeps him from time to time because she chose to be a part of his life from the start.* That's how it sounded to Mackenzie.

Ellington brought in the cake and started slicing. When he gave Kevin a little piece, he responded by promptly slamming his hand down onto it and giggling. This elicited laughter from both grandmothers which, in turn, resulted in another attack on the cake from Kevin.

"Wait now," Patricia said. "Isn't he too young for cake like that?"

"No," Mackenzie said. "Kevin loves ice cream."

"I don't remember ever giving you ice cream that young."

Mackenzie thought, but did not dare say: *I'm surprised you remember much of anything from my childhood.*

"Oh yeah," Frances said. "He especially loves strawberry ice cream. But not chocolate. You should see the yucky faces this kid makes when he tries anything chocolate."

Mackenzie watched her mother's face and saw the ghost of the woman she had once been. There was disappointment there, and a look of embarrassment. She instantly started to straighten her posture into a defensive stance and Mackenzie knew right away that things were going to get dicey if they continued on this way.

"Don't worry, though, Mom," Mackenzie said. "He gets plenty of healthy stuff, too."

"I wasn't questioning, I was just ... curious. It's been a while since I raised a child ..."

"Isn't it odd?" Frances said. "You think you're done with being ensnared by the magic of children when your own leave home and then ... *bam!* You're a grandparent."

"It is, I suppose," Patricia said, looking at Kevin. She reached out with one hand and he grasped it, coating her index finger in vanilla ice cream.

"As you can see," Frances said, "he's quite good at sharing, too."

Patricia chuckled at this, a noise that earned a big smile from Kevin. Mackenzie could see the tears in her mother's eyes, but she continued to laugh all the same. And by the time her laughter was at a fever pitch, Kevin was cackling right along with her, as if they had just shared a very private joke.

"I assume he gets his sense of humor from your side of the family," Frances said. "God knows my kids were never much for laughter."

"Hey," Ellington said. "A lot of people happen to think I'm funny! Right, Mac?"

"I don't know," she said. "Have I ever met any of them?"

He rolled his eyes at her as their mothers had a laugh at his expense. Kevin joined in again, continuing to slap at the ice cream cake as he shoved some into his mouth.

It's like the twilight zone, Mackenzie thought as she watched the entire exchange. Their mothers were actually getting along. And it wasn't forced. Sure, it had only been a few moments but something about it felt natural. Something about it—God help her—felt *right.*

She was sure she was staring, but she couldn't help it. And there was no telling how long she might have kept staring if the phone had not rung and broken her out of it. She jumped at the chance to get away from the table, hurrying to her phone on the kitchen counter without even wondering who it might be.

That all changed when she saw Director McGrath's name on the caller ID screen. It was after five in the afternoon and whenever McGrath called at such a time, it usually meant she was going to have a busy few days on her hands. She picked up the phone and looked through the entryway into the dining area, hoping to lock eyes with Ellington. As it was, though, he was speaking to his mother and cleaning up some of the ice cream from Kevin's hands and face.

"This is Agent White," she answered.

"Hey, White." McGrath's voice was somber as always. It was hard to tell his mood by those two simple words. "I believe I have a case that might be tailor made for you. It's sort of a rush, though. I'd need to you get prepped tonight and be on a plane very early tomorrow morning, headed for Utah."

"That's fine, but why aren't local agents out there handling it?"

"It's a special circumstance. I'll explain it all when you get to my office. How soon can you and Ellington get here?"

She was a little disappointed in herself to be so relieved to have an easy out—a viable excuse to step away from this weirdness with her mother and Frances.

"Soon, actually," she said. "We sort of have a built-in babysitter at the moment."

"Excellent. Half an hour work for you?"

"That's perfect," she said. She ended the call and then, still staring into the dining area and trying to make sense of it all, she called out: "Hey, E? Can you come here a second?"

Perhaps it was the tone in her voice or the simple deduction that no one ever called them other than people they worked with, but Ellington came right away, and with an expectant smile on his face.

"Work?" he asked.

"Yeah."

"Great," Ellington said. "Because quite frankly, whatever is going on in there is just straight up weird."

"I know, right?"

Then, as if to punctuate this, both of their mothers chuckled at something from the dining room, and it was followed by their son's bright cackling laughter.

CHAPTER FOUR

While it felt odd to leave Kevin with *both* grandmothers, Mackenzie could not deny that it did her heart some good to know that her mother was finally getting in some quality time with her son. Her only fear was that her mother's stubborn and rather selfish side would pop up and get defensive when it became clear that Kevin and Frances had already formed something of a bond. She was astounded that there were no worries about the situation as she and Ellington made their way through the emptying halls of FBI headquarters to McGrath's office.

When they entered, it was clear that he was shutting things down for the day. He was placing a few folders into his briefcase and seemed to be in a rather chipper mood.

"Thanks for coming on such short notice," he said.

"No problem," Ellington said. "You actually sort of did us a favor."

"Is that so?"

"Extended family stuff," Mackenzie said.

"None of my business then. So I'll make this short and sweet. We have a dead woman out in Utah. The bureau was called in on it because as far as local law enforcement can tell, the woman has no identity. No records, no social security number, no birth certificate, no known addresses, nothing."

"And why call agents in DC to handle it rather than field agents in Salt Lake City?" Mackenzie asked.

"I don't know all of the details, but the bureau down there is in a bit of a pickle. Due to some past issues in the area with certain protected individuals, the Salt Lake City branch has to be incredibly careful about how they handle investigations in the area."

"That's rather vague," Ellington said.

"Well, it's all I have for you right now. I can also offer that there was a conflict of interest and after things went to court, the bureau ended up being in the wrong. So the Salt Lake City heads called us today to see if we could get some DC agents out there on it to work discreetly. And given the nature of the killing, it seemed like something the two of you would knock out rather easily. Get down there, figure out who she is and who killed her. And why. Then hand it over to the local police and come back home."

"And what *is* the nature of the murder?" Ellington asked.

"I'll have the full reports emailed to you. But it appears that this young woman was running away from someone late at night. The working assumption is that while she was running, she was struck by a vehicle and then had her throat cut. There was also a strip of tape placed across her mouth but the medical examiner thinks it was done after the death."

Mackenzie figured it *was* right up their alley. She wasn't sure how to feel about that.

"When do you need us out there?" Ellington asked.

"There are flights booked for both of you at five fifteen tomorrow morning. I'd like to have you on that flight and looking at the crime scene by noon tomorrow. I know childcare might be an issue for a case like this one, but—"

"For once, I think that might be taken care of," Ellington said.

"Wait. I don't know if—"

"Is this the extended family stuff?" McGrath asked. He was done packing up, looking longingly at the door.

"Yes, sir."

"Like I said, then. None of my business. If there's a problem with childcare and only one of you can go, let me know."

And with that said, he pointed them toward the door.

"I'll just say it," Mackenzie said on the way back to the apartment. "I wasn't overly comfortable with your mom keeping Kevin the last time we were on a case. A few hours here and there, absolutely. I'm fine with it. But for several days . . ."

"Oh, I feel you on that. But, if we're speaking candidly, the thought of leaving him with *your* mother for a few days doesn't make me feel warm and safe, either."

"Oh, God no."

"If you're really bothered by the idea of my mother keeping him, I can be the dutiful husband and just stay back. Sounds like a pretty basic job out there and—"

"No. McGrath actually asked us *both* to run this. As a team. Three months ago, he thought pairing us was a bad idea, so we must be doing something right. If he's giving us this chance, I think we need to take it."

"I agree," Ellington said.

"So what do we do?"

They were quiet for a moment, but then Ellington spoke up. When he did, he spoke slowly, as if making sure every word was right—or that he actually meant what he was saying. "What's the likelihood of them being here at the same time?" he said. "Really, think about that. The chances are incredibly slim. And if neither of us trusts one of them individually..."

"You mean you want them to tag-team babysitting?"

"It could work. You saw how they were getting along. And my God, Kevin looked like he was in grandma heaven."

"Will your mom get offended?" she asked.

"I doubt it. Will yours?"

"No. Hell, she'll be flattered that I'm asking her such a thing. Did you see the look on her face when I told her you and I had to head out for a quick meeting and were trusting them to watch over him?"

"Yeah, I did." He considered it for a while as they came to the intersection where they would turn left to reach their apartment. "So...if the place isn't burned down when we get back, do we want to ask both of them?"

Mackenzie panicked at the thought for only a moment. She recalled the brief visit she'd had with her mother months ago—how her mother had finally started getting back on her feet and acting responsibly. Maybe her visit out here and the desire to finally see her grandson was the turning point. And if Mackenzie could make sure her mother kept heading in the right direction, wasn't it her responsibility as a daughter to make sure it happened? Certainly a few days with a thirteen-month-old grandson would help.

As they stepped onto the elevator in their building, Mackenzie reached out and took Ellington's hand. "You okay with this? You sure?"

He made a confused expression while he nodded. "I am. I know it's weird, but yeah. I think it will be okay. You?"

"Same."

They entered the apartment, returning about eighty minutes after they had walked out. They found Frances wiping down the kitchen counters while Patricia sat on the floor playing with Kevin. They were currently playing with his Spin 'n' Speak, one of his favorite toys. Seeing her mother down on the floor playing with him warmed her heart in a way that she had not expected. She gave Ellington a little nudge into the living room as they came through the door, indicating that he was going to have to be the one to do the speaking.

"So . . . Mom? Ms. White?"

"Oh, no, Patricia, please."

"Okay . . . Mom and Patricia. So, Mackenzie and I have just been given an opportunity to work together on a case. We have before, of course, but ever since we got married, the bureau has been a little weird about pairing us up. But this time, it was requested."

"Well, that's wonderful," Frances said.

"It is. Only, the case is in Utah. And we need to be on a plane around five o'clock in the morning."

Patricia looked up at them for the first time since they had come in; her attention had been on Kevin the entire time. "Anything dangerous?" she asked.

"No more than usual," Mackenzie said. "But we're mentioning this to both of you because we understand just how unlikely it is that you're both here. So, Mom . . . you had planned on staying in town for two days, right?"

"Yes, that's right."

"And you," Ellington said, pointing to his mother, "showed up unannounced, which makes me think you have no plans anytime soon. Is that a safe assumption?"

"I had planned to go home tomorrow, but I have no concrete plans, no."

"Any chance you can cancel your hotel room and get a refund, Mom?" Mackenzie asked.

Patricia seemed to understand where this was going. She looked to Kevin, smiled brightly, and then back to her daughter with a bit of apprehension. "Mackenzie . . . I don't know. I want to, sure. Of course I do. But are *you* sure?"

"It would be both of you," Mackenzie said. "If Frances is up for it. Two or three days at most, I would think. Are you both okay with that?"

The tears that leaked from her mother's eyes was all the answer Mackenzie needed. Still, Patricia nodded and got to her feet. When she came over and hugged her daughter, Mackenzie barely knew what to do. She hugged her mother back, unsure what it meant that it felt a little forced and awkward. Had it really been *that* long since they had embraced out of emotion rather than social necessity?

"Count me in, too," Frances said. "I only have enough clothes for a day or two, but I can do the wash."

"Mackenzie, I don't even know where to start," Patricia said. "It's been so long since I cared for a baby and . . ."

"It's like riding a bike," Frances assured her. "And little Kevin there is an angel. Not a problem at all."

"And we'll leave a schedule for you," Mackenzie said.

"As well as the numbers for the doctor, fire department, and poison control," Ellington quipped.

When no one laughed, he grimaced and slowly stepped out of the room. Kevin, sitting on the floor, provided the only response as he craned his neck to see where his daddy was going.

"Think you can handle it, kiddo?" Mackenzie asked, getting down on the floor with him.

His only response was his usual smile and his big bright eyes as he looked up at his mother and the two older women behind her.

CHAPTER FIVE

About halfway through their flight to Utah, Mackenzie was on her second cup of bitter airline coffee as her first signs of worry took root. She glanced out the window, the early morning light blooming over the horizon, and then to Ellington.

"Still feel good about it?" she asked him.

"I do. Why? You changing your mind?"

"No. I just know my mother. I mean, it's obvious she's changing her life for the better and I hope spending some time with Kevin only helps to super-charge those changes. But I know my mother. I know how stubborn she can be. I know how defensive she can be. I can't help but wonder if our mothers together might turn into a WWE cage match."

"As long as they keep Kevin alive, I'm fine with that. I'd put my money on your mom, by the way."

She could tell that he was slightly worried, but was trying to be the strong husband that she could depend on. Throughout their marriage and the years of partnering together beforehand, he had learned when to take on that role and when to step back and let her be strong. He was getting very good at doing both and knowing which role to fill at the appropriate time. She sighed, looked back out the window, and held his hand.

"Hey, Mac? It really is okay. It's going to be great. This is part of being a family, you know? In-laws, relatives, all of it."

"I know. But today it's my mom. Tomorrow, what if my sister wants to step up and be an aunt all of a sudden?"

"Then you have to let her. Or, at the very least, let her try."

"Oh, but you haven't met Stephanie . . ."

"And I hadn't met your mother until yesterday. Yet here we are, in the sky while she and my mother are down below, taking care of our son. And if I can be honest...?"

"Please do."

"I think you're worried about it because you *aren't* worried about it. You and I were both rocked by how natural it felt. Maybe we just need to go with it and focus on this case. Our mothers raised us and we turned out fine, after all."

"Did we, though?" she asked with a smirk.

"Eh, good enough."

Mackenzie continued to sip from her coffee and did exactly what Ellington had suggested, turning her thoughts away from the surprising result back home and toward the case.

They drove their rental car sixteen miles outside of Salt Lake City, on task to beat McGrath's projection of a noon arrival by nearly an hour. The town where the woman without an identity had been murdered was a cute little place called Fellsburg. It was a slightly upscale town, likely the sort of town that thrived only because it was so close to Salt Lake City. Mackenzie imagined most of the population made that commute daily, working in the city and then coming back to their homes in one of the numerous neighborhoods in Fellsburg.

Following the file notes and instructions in the information McGrath had emailed to them, Ellington drove them to a subdivision called Plainsview. It looked like the two other subdivisions they had to pass to get there—two-story houses, cookie-cutouts of one another. Nice trimmed yards, security streetlights every one hundred feet or so.

But they didn't have to venture far into Plainsview. Four houses after the entrance, there was a cop car parked on the side of the street. This was the officer who had arranged to meet with them when Mackenzie had called from the airport to announce their arrival. He was already getting out of his patrol car when Ellington pulled in behind him.

The three of them met between the cars, going through a round of introductions. The badge and pin he wore on his chest indicated he was Sheriff Burke.

"Agents," Burke said. "Thanks for coming out. I'm Sheriff Declan Burke."

Mackenzie and Ellington gave their names, shaking hands with him. Mackenzie guessed Burke to be about fifty or so. He had a thick beard that could use a trim and a hardened face. His eyes were hidden behind a pair of aviator sunglasses even though the morning was not bright at all.

"This is where the body was discovered?" Mackenzie asked.

"It is. Right there." Burke pointed to a spot just slightly right of center.

"According to the report, there was nothing on her except a driver's license, correct?"

"That, and a pair of sandals. They were wet from the little bit of rain we had gotten that day. She wasn't wearing the sandals, though. At first, I thought the car knocked her out of them, but the MD pointed out that there were cuts and abrasions on her feet that indicated she took them off in the hopes of maybe running faster."

"Any idea how far she had been running?" Ellington asked.

"We're not really clear on that," Burke said. "There's a field about a mile and a half away from here that shows some signs of someone passing through that same night. But the growth of weeds and wild grass makes it impossible to tell for sure if it was this woman—or even a human being at all. Could have been a deer or something."

"And no one around here saw anything?" Mackenzie asked. She looked down the street, to the slightly sloping road and the nice homes. There were plenty of streetlights. It was hard to believe no one had seen anything.

"My men and I questioned every homeowner on this street. We have one night owl who claims to have seen an old town car driving through the neighborhood with its lights off. But they didn't get a plate number."

"And what about the girl?" Ellington said. "No known identity at all?"

"None that we can find. The driver's license was a fake. And a damned convincing one at that. We of course took her fingerprints and drew blood. None of them match to anyone in the system."

"That makes no sense," Ellington commented.

"And that's why we called you guys out here," Burke said. "You saw the pictures of the body at the scene, I assume?"

"Yes," Mackenzie said. "Black duct tape over her mouth. The ME believes it was placed there postmortem."

19

"That's right. Checked the tape for prints and got nothing."

Mackenzie had studied that strip of tape in the photographs for a while last night and on the plane this morning. She figured it could be symbolic, some way of the killer letting the woman know even in death that she needed to be quiet. But why? What did she have to say?

"With no identity, I guess it's been next to impossible to identify friends or family members," Ellington said.

"Yeah. We have *nothing*. So I will now gladly hand this over to you. Need anything from me?"

"Yes, actually," Mackenzie said. "No prints were found on the driver's license?"

"Just the girl's."

"What's the forensics lab like at your station?"

"Not state of the art by any means, but better than most in towns of this size."

"Get your forensics guys to take a closer look at that license. Check it under a microscope with ultraviolet light. Some forgers put a little signature or mark on their work. It's always hidden well, but sometimes it's *there*. Sort of a sneaky little middle-finger to people like us."

"I'll do that," Burke said. "Anything else?"

Mackenzie was about to ask Ellington what he thought, but she was interrupted by the ringing of her phone. It was on silent, but they could all hear it buzzing from inside her coat pocket. She turned away and pulled the phone out of her pocket. She was irritated and a little alarmed to see it was her mother. She nearly ignored it but the thought of her and Frances keeping Kevin sat heavy on her mind.

She took a few steps away and answered the call, already dreading the news that may be waiting on the other end.

"Hey, Mom. Is everything okay?"

"Yes, everything is good. Kevin is perfectly fine."

"So then why the call? You know I'm right at the start of case, right?"

"I do. But I just need to know something. Is Frances always this overbearing?"

"How do you mean?"

"Just being bossy. I know she's been around Kevin more than I have but she's acting like she knows every single detail about him, and questioning everything I do."

"That's why you're calling me?"

"Yes. I'm sorry, Mackenzie, I just—"

"Both of you are big girls. You'll find a way to work together. For now, I have to go. Please, Mom . . . don't call me again unless it's urgent."

"Okay." There was hurt and disappointment in her voice, but Mackenzie looked past it.

She killed the call and turned back to Ellington and Burke. Burke looked at her almost apologetically as he headed back to his patrol car. "I was just telling your partner here that we've got an office space set up for you guys back at the station. I've got a few other things I need to check on, so just make yourselves at home. And feel free to call me directly if anything pressing pops up."

He seemed relieved to be leaving the scene as he got into his car. He gave them a little wave before he pulled off, leaving them to look at the section of road where the mystery woman had been killed.

"Important call?" Ellington asked.

"It was my mother."

"Oh? Everything okay?"

"Yes. She was just calling to let me know the cage match is officially underway."

CHAPTER SIX

The first thing Mackenzie did when they arrived at the station was to go through the physical records to get actual photos of the crime scene rather than the digital ones she and Ellington had been given. She spread them out on the large table that took up most of their designated office space and hunched over them for a moment. As she studied them, Ellington started taking down notes on his phone.

The girl was rather young. Mackenzie doubted she was older than twenty. She was blonde and had a face that most would consider pretty. But there was some quality to her, even in her emotionless dead face, that made Mackenzie think the girl may have been a runaway or a vagrant. That, or she'd been through some trauma recently. Her skin simply had a pallor to it that spoke of grime and hard living.

"No identity," she said, speaking to herself more than to Ellington. "I wonder if she was from WITSEC."

"Witness protection?" Ellington said. "That's a bit of a leap. Especially with a license you think might be a fake."

"Well, she has no real ID and she was running hard from someone. If she was with witness protection *and* on the run, that would give us at least somewhere to start looking. Maybe someone from her past found her."

"That's why I love you," Ellington said. "You'd rather look hard at a theory without legs than admit you have nowhere to start."

"There's always somewhere to start," Mackenzie said, still eyeing the photos. "It's just that sometimes the place you start is the hardest."

She pulled out her phone, her eyes bouncing back and forth between her contacts and the pictures of the dead girl on the table.

"Who you calling?" Ellington asked.

"I'm going to have DC patch me through to the US Marshals office to see if they'll get me a list."

Ellington, clearly surprised by the suggestion, nodded comically. "Yeah, good luck with that."

As the phone was answered and she was placed on hold and then finally patched through to the Marshals office, she continued to eye the pictures. The injuries sustained by the vehicle striking her weren't obvious in the pictures, but the harsh slit across her throat was glaring. The pavement in the pictures was slightly wet and glistening, making the dark red coming from her neck almost surreal.

"This is Assistant Chief Manning," a rough voice said through the other end of the phone. "Who is this?"

"This is Special Agent Mackenzie White, with the FBI. I'm working a case in Salt Lake City that I believe may involve a young woman out of WITSEC. We have absolutely no ID. Her prints aren't in any database and the driver's license found on her body is a fake. I'm taking a shot in the dark and hoping she might be in your system."

"Agent White, you know I can't give you the identities of people under our security. That would be breaking about a dozen different laws and regulations."

"I'm aware of that. But what if I sent you a picture? Using facial recognition, you could maybe come up with something and—"

"Pardon me, but even if you only *suspect* she might be with WITSEC, sending a picture back and forth breaks even more rules."

"Being that it's a crime scene photo, I think it's permissible," Mackenzie snapped. "She was hit by a vehicle and then had her throat slit. So I'm not sending you a glamour shot."

Manning gave a deep sigh that indicated Mackenzie was about to get her way. "Send the picture over and I'll have someone run a facial recognition search. Of course, I can't promise anything. But I'll see what we can do."

"Thanks."

"We'll get back to you as soon as we can." He gave her the information of where to send the picture before hanging up.

Ellington had been looking over the coroner's report while she spoke with Manning. "Got your way, huh?"

"Was there ever any doubt?"

He shook his head and handed the coroner's report over to her. "This is the most recent, fresh off the presses about five hours ago. Sort of interesting, don't you think?"

She scanned the report, looking over the obvious content until she came to the most recent updates. What she found did indeed seem interesting. According to the most recent updates from the coroner and the medical examiner, it appeared that the victim had suffered several broken bones in the past that had not healed correctly. Two ribs, the left wrist, and a buckle fracture along her right arm. According to the coroner's notes, the bones of the left wrist looked as if they had never been properly set at all.

"You thinking domestic abuse?" Mackenzie asked.

"I think she was running away from someone and she had a history of broken bones that weren't set. So yeah...domestic abuse and maybe even something darker. I wonder if she was maybe held captive. She doesn't look the healthiest, you know. The report has her listed as weighing one hundred and fifteen pounds. And you can see it in her face in the pictures...she looks sort of...I don't know..."

"Hardened," Mackenzie finished for him.

"Yeah, that's a good word for it."

"So maybe she was a prisoner or captive and she managed to get away from her abuser. And when he caught up to her, he figured it was going to be easier to kill her rather than capture her again."

"But for someone to be so carefree about that, it would mean the abuser must have known she had no identity."

It was a good point, one that left them in silence to mull it over individually. Mackenzie thought of a girl, potentially running through a damp field and then down a rain-slicked road. She had been barefoot, apparently carrying her sandals. The scenario presented two questions, but she wasn't sure which one was more important.

The first was where was she running away from?

The second, as she pondered it, started to seem more pressing. "Where was she going?" Mackenzie asked out loud. "It can't be a coincidence that she chose that neighborhood. I know there is no evidence that it was her that ran through the field Sheriff Burke mentioned, but what if she did? She could have gone in any direction and chosen any neighborhood. So why that one?"

Ellington smiled as he nodded, catching on to her enthusiasm. "Why don't we go find out?"

CHAPTER SEVEN

They were fortunate in that it was a Saturday and most of the cars within the neighborhood were parked in driveways or opened garages. They arrived back in the Plainsview neighborhood at 3:10, parking in the same spot they had met Sheriff Burke. It was a sunny March afternoon, not quite chilly but certainly not warm either. Regardless, Mackenzie did not expect to have much of a problem finding people to speak with.

"You take the right, I'll take the left," Ellington said as they got out of the car.

Mackenzie nodded, knowing that most partners opted not to take the split-up approach. But she and Ellington trusted one another on a level that allowed for this. It came not only in their strong work partnership, but from the bonds of marriage as well. They separated without any fanfare and took their respective sides of the street.

The first house on Mackenzie's side was a no-brainer, as a mother and her daughter were in the front yard. The daughter was maybe six years old, pedaling a Little Tikes tricycle up and down the sidewalk. The mother was sitting on the porch, scrolling on her phone. When Mackenzie approached, she looked up and offered a smile.

"Can I help you?" she asked. Her tone indicated she did not want to help at all, especially if Mackenzie was selling something.

Mackenzie got a little farther away from the little girl before she pulled her badge and introduced herself. "I'm Agent Mackenzie White, with the FBI. My partner and I are scouring the neighborhood to see if we can find out any information on the hit-and-run from two nights ago."

"Nope," she said. "I told the cops the same thing. The way they tell it, they think it happened after midnight, and everyone in my home is asleep by eleven."

"Do you happen to know who found the body?"

"Not for sure. There's all sorts of rumors circulating and I don't know which ones to believe. After a while, I just topped paying attention to them, you know?"

"Any of it coming from people you would trust with information like that?"

"I'm afraid not."

"Well, thanks for your time."

She turned away and gave the little girl a wave as she made her way to the next house over. She knocked three times but got no answer. She received the same result at the third house. The fourth home was different. The door was answered right after she rang the doorbell.

Mackenzie found herself looking at an older lady, maybe just a little shy of sixty. She was carrying a bottle of Pledge and a duster. Some '70s rock was playing behind her; Peter Frampton, if Mackenzie's rather impressive musical knowledge was correct. She was clearly distracted by her cleaning, but greeted Mackenzie with a smile anyway.

"Sorry to bother you," Mackenzie said. "I'm Agent White, FBI." She flashed her badge and the woman looked at it as if Mackenzie had just performed a magic trick. "I'm canvassing the neighborhood to find any information I can on the hit-and-run that occurred on your street two nights ago."

"Oh, of course," the woman said. And just like that, her cleaning was forgotten. "Have you found who was responsible?"

"Not yet. That's why we're here, trying to find some leads. Did you happen to see or hear anything that night?"

"No. I don't know that anyone did. And that's the scariest thing of all."

"How's that?"

"Well, it's a very peaceful neighborhood. But we're also sort of out in the middle of nowhere. Sure, Salt Lake City is less than twenty miles away, but as you can see, we don't really have that big-city feel out here."

"What sort of gossip has been circling?" Mackenzie asked.

"None that I'm aware of. It's too dark of a thing to talk about." She took a step through the doorway, closer to Mackenzie so she could speak in a conspiratorial tone. "I get the feeling that most everyone in this neighborhood believes that by not talking about it, the whole thing will just go away—that everyone will forget about it."

Mackenzie nodded. She'd worked cases in several towns like this. However, she also knew that it was in those small neighborhoods where gossip tended to plant its roots and really start to grow.

But as her trip down the street continued, she wasn't so sure that was going to be the case in Plainsview. There were two basic attitudes among the residents: those who were irritated with the FBI visiting because they had already spoken to the police, and those who were genuinely afraid for the state of their neighborhood now that the bureau was involved.

The eighth house she came to was rather unremarkable. There were no flowers in the flowerbeds, just used up mulch that had long ago gone discolored. While there was furniture on the porch, it was also in a state of disrepair, one of the chairs festooned with cobwebs. Two houses shy of the first intersection in the neighborhood, it didn't quite stick out but Mackenzie guessed that some of the older property owners might frown upon this home.

She knocked on the door and heard the slight shuffling of footsteps inside. Another ten seconds passed before anyone came to the door. And when they did, it was opened only a crack. A young woman peered out, her dark eyes taking in the sight of Mackenzie with the sort of scrutiny that suggested she was a suspicious woman.

"Yeah?" the young woman asked.

Mackenzie showed her badge and ID, instantly getting a strange vibe from this woman. Everyone else had opened their doors wide, yet this woman looked as if she was using her door as a shield. Perhaps she was one of the residents who had opted for a reaction of absolute fear in response to the murder.

"I'm Agent White, with the FBI. I was hoping to ask you some questions about the hit-and-run that occurred here two nights ago."

"Me?" the woman asked, confused.

"No, not just you. My partner and I are going door to door to ask all residents. Please forgive me for asking, but you look a little young. Are your parents home?"

A quick flicker of irritation crossed the woman's face. "I'm twenty years old," she said. "I live here with my two roommates."

"Oh, my apologies. So...do you recall anything interesting about that night?"

"No. I mean, from what I gather, it happened very late. I'm usually asleep by ten or eleven."

"And you heard nothing?"

"No."

The woman was still not opening the door all the way. She was also speaking quite fast. Mackenzie didn't think the woman was hiding something, but she was behaving in a way that made Mackenzie start to wonder.

"What's your name?" she asked.

"Amy Campbell."

"Amy, are your roommates home?"

"One of them is. The other is out running errands."

"Do you know if they saw or heard anything out of the ordinary on the night of the hit-and-run?"

"They didn't. We all talked about it, trying to figure it out. But we were all asleep by ten thirty that night."

Mackenzie nearly asked to come inside, but decided not to. Amy was clearly freaked out about the situation and there was no sense in making it any worse. As the tense moment passed between them, Mackenzie caught motion behind Amy. Another woman was walking down the hallway and taking a left into another room. She looked to be about Amy's age and had an angular face. Her hair, which appeared to be brown, was up in a messy bun. Mackenzie almost asked who this was but sensed that if she did, she might lose any traction she was building with Amy.

"How did you hear about the murder?" Mackenzie asked.

"From the police. They came by, doing exactly what you're doing, that morning."

"And you told them exactly what you're telling me?"

"Yes. Honestly, I saw nothing. Heard nothing. I wish I could help because it's just awful . . . but I was asleep."

It was in that comment that Mackenzie detected some emotion. Amy was either sad or in a state of despair about something—which made sense, given what had happened on her very street just two nights ago. Still, she was acting much stranger than anyone else she had spoken with. Mackenzie reached into her inner coat pocket and took out one of her business cards. When she handed it over to Amy, the young woman took it quickly.

"Please call me if you or your roommates happen to think of anything—or if you even hear some of your neighbors mention anything strange. Can you do that?"

"Yes. Good luck, Agent."

Amy Campbell quickly shut the door, leaving Mackenzie standing alone on the dirty porch. She walked back down the porch steps slowly, thinking a few things over.

A twenty-year-old renting a house in a neighborhood like this . . . that's sort of strange. But if she has roommates, there could be a chance they are college students at some college in Salt Lake City. Maybe it's cheaper and nicer than on-campus housing.

While the whole situation did seem a bit strange, she had to remind herself that a brutal murder had happened on this street. People were going to handle it differently—especially college-aged girls who knew the victim had been right around their age.

Mackenzie worked it all out in her head as she stepped back toward the street. As she did, she passed the two cars sitting on the little concrete slab that was Amy Campbell's driveway. They were both rather old, one being at 2005 Pontiac that looked like it might fall apart the next time it hit a pothole.

Before heading further down the street. Mackenzie took her phone out. She typed in Amy's name and the address for future reference. It was just a hunch but more often than not, Mackenzie's hunches paid off in the end.

She tucked her phone back into her pocket and headed further down the street to knock on more doors.

CHAPTER EIGHT

Eight minutes and three houses later, Mackenzie's trek of the Plainsview subdivision was interrupted by a phone call. Sheriff Burke was on the other end, his voice somehow rougher through the phone. He had one of those expressionless voices that made it pretty much impossible to tell what sort of mood he was in.

"Just got a call from the forensics lab. They didn't find any sort of hidden signature under the UV light. But they did find a partial thumbprint that did not belong to the girl."

"Any results come up from it?"

"Yeah, I just ran it. The print belongs to a guy named Todd Thompson. I've got an officer running a check on him right now."

"So, no signature at all … which means there's a good chance the license is legitimately made."

"Still makes no sense. The name on the license matches nothing in our records. Neither do her fingerprints. If the picture on the license didn't look almost exactly like her, I'd say she stole it from somewhere."

"I suppose we could run a search for women who placed reports in regards to losing their purses or licenses in the last month or so."

"We already did that on the first day. Got a few nibbles, but nothing panned out. We also tried to … hold on, I've got an officer here with results on Todd Thompson. Gonna put you on speaker, Agent White."

There was some shuffling, a clicking noise, and then another voice. This was a female voice, just as stern as Burke's but with more emotion. There was excitement in her tone as she perhaps suspected what she was saying might very well lead them toward the end of this case.

"A basic state records search shows that Todd Thompson is a native of Salt Lake City. He's fifty-three years old and—get this—works at the DMV."

The DMV connection certainly shed new light on the bizarre driver's license. Mackenzie could nearly hear the clinking of gears in her head as it all came into place.

"Got a home address?"

"I do. I'll scan this report and send it to you as soon as we hang up."

"Perfect."

They ended the call and Mackenzie looked down the street, back the way she had come. The site of the hit-and-run was now out of sight, about six houses down and on a completely different block. She looked over and saw that Ellington was one house ahead of her. He was currently speaking to an older gentleman through an opened door. She was pretty sure he'd be more than happy to end this door-to-door task.

She hurried across the street to give him the latest update as a chilled afternoon breeze swept through the neighborhood.

According to the report Burke and his officer sent over, Todd Thompson had a few minor dings on his record. Two unpaid parking tickets (which Mackenzie found somewhat funny, considering his occupation), and a charge of aiding a breaking and entering from nearly thirty years ago. Other than that, Todd Thompson looked squeaky clean. Except for the fact that his thumbprint had been lightly placed on the presumably fake driver's license of a woman who appeared to have no identity.

Mackenzie shared all of this with Ellington as he drove them into the city. She also shared her peculiar encounter with Amy Campbell. As it turned out, it was the most interesting visit out of their combined nineteen homes. Ellington agreed that Amy's mood could have simply been a reflection of a woman her own age being killed less than a thousand feet away from her front door.

By the time they entered the city and were headed for Todd Thompson's residence, they both felt that this could be the visit that sealed the case. Mackenzie did not say anything out loud about it, but she was anxious to get back home. The single call from her mother had upset her more than she was willing to admit and she suddenly felt foolish for thinking her mother would be able to keep a child without somehow making it all about her.

Night was just beginning to fall when Ellington parked the car in front of Thompson's apartment building. He lived in one of the nicer areas of the city, the apartment building located on a corner that looked out over a small park and a square where it looked as if farmer's markets and crafts fairs were set up on the weekend. As they entered, a few of the vendors were just finishing packing up for the day.

When Mackenzie knocked on the door of the second-floor apartment, she wondered how many doors she had knocked on today. Eleven? Twelve? She wasn't sure.

"One minute," a man's cheerful voice called from the other side. When the door was finally opened, they were greeted by not only a middle-aged African American man, but the smell of Thai food as well.

"Are you Mr. Todd Thompson?" Ellington asked.

"That's me," he said. He looked confused at first, but when he saw both agents reaching for their badges, a look of understanding fell across his face. Seeing that expression, Mackenzie realized that Mr. Thompson had been expecting this visit for quite some time.

"We're with the FBI," Mackenzie said. "We're looking into the murder of a young woman about twenty miles north of here. Given that your fingerprint showed up on her license, I'd appreciate it if we could come inside."

Thompson nodded, stepping aside and allowing them in. Now, more than ever, Mackenzie was sure he had known this day was coming. Oddly enough, he didn't seem all that scared. This was further proven when, after he closed the door behind them, he immediately went to the small table in the kitchen and sat down behind his Thai takeout.

"Forgive me for saying so," Mackenzie said, "but you don't seem all that upset to have the FBI showing up at your door."

"With proof that you handled a now-dead woman's driver's license at that," Ellington added.

"When was she killed?" Thompson asked. He did sound sad, and his eyes started to grow distant as he ate his dinner.

"You honestly don't know who we're talking about?"

"No. But I know about the licenses."

"Plural?" Mackenzie asked.

Thompson took one last bite, then dropped the plastic fork into the food and slid the plate away from him. He sighed deeply and looked at the agents with sad eyes. "Yeah," he said. "There's probably quite a few of them floating around."

"You're not making sense, Mr. Thompson," Mackenzie said. "Why don't you tell us why your thumbprint appeared on a dead woman's fake license?"

"Because I made it. Though I used a powder when making them that was supposed to keep my prints off of them. You use UV?"

"We did."

"Shit. Well, yeah ... I made the license."

"At the DMV, I assume?" Mackenzie asked.

"Yes."

"Did the young woman pay you for it? The name on the license was Marjorie Hikkum."

"No. It's always the same woman that pays for them."

Mackenzie was starting to get irritated with the cavalier nature in which Thompson was explaining things. She could tell by the way Ellington's jaw was set that he was getting mad, too.

"Mr. Thompson, please explain what the hell you're talking about."

"I've been doing it for about three years now. This woman comes in, pretends to have some sort of issue, and slides me some money. Five hundred bucks per ID. A week later, I give her what she asked for."

"You understand how highly illegal that is, right?" Ellington asked.

"I do. But this woman ... she's trying to do some good. She gets these IDs because she's trying to help those girls."

"What girls?" Ellington asked, almost barking the question.

Thompson looked at them, confused. It took him a moment to understand what was happening and then he gave them an apologetic look. "Damn. I'm sorry. If you were here asking about the IDs and a dead woman, I figured you probably already knew. The IDs I make are for women that manage to escape that crazy-farm on the other side of Fellsburg."

"What crazy-farm?" Mackenzie asked.

This question made Thompson look genuinely worried for the first time since they had knocked on his door. He made a slight grimace and shook his head softly. "I don't feel right talking about it. Too much power up there, you know?"

"No, we don't know." Though she did remember McGrath stating that there was some sort of religious community in the area, which was one of the reasons the local agents were jumping at the case.

"Well, Mr. Thompson, I hate to play it this way," Ellington said, "but you already fessed up to making fake IDs. If we wanted, we could arrest you for that and make sure you spend at least six months in a federal prison. Depending on who you sold them to, it could be worse than that. However, if you can let us know about the women these IDs are for and it helps us with this case, then we can sort of wave that away. We'd insist that you stop creating fake documents at a government facility like the DMV, but that would be it."

Thompson looked a little embarrassed that he had even fallen into such a trap. The pained look on his face dissolved into a defeated grin. "Any way you can keep my name out of it?"

"Unless there are extenuating circumstances, I don't see why not," Mackenzie said. "Are you afraid someone may seek some kind of revenge?"

"With these people, I just don't know." When he saw that the agents still had no clear idea of what he was talking about, he sighed again and went on. "This woman comes in and buys the IDs. She gets them for women that are trying to escape the Community. They use them to get back on their feet—just some small thing they can possess that helps them start a new life. A normal life."

"What's the Community?" Ellington asked.

"A religious commune about fifteen miles on the other side of Fellsburg— about forty minutes away from here. A lot of people know about it, but no one really talks about it. When they do, it's either in a joking way or in a spooky campfire sort of way."

"Any idea why women that join this Community would need to escape it?"

Thompson shrugged. "I don't know for sure. And that's the truth. Honestly, I don't know much more about the place than anyone else you'd pull off the street. I just make and sell those IDs."

"You know nothing about what they practice?"

"Rumor has it that it's some sort of polygamist cult. Some of the men are supposed to have like three or four wives. They're supposed to very religious— very Old Testament wrath-type stuff."

"And what about this woman that buys the IDs from you? What do you know about her?"

"Not too much. When she came in and asked if I wanted the side gig, one of the things she said was that I couldn't ask questions. I thought it was bullshit but then she slid me five hundred bucks. And look...I'm damn near sixty and still in debt. I can't pass up that kind of money."

"You don't even know her name?" Ellington asked.

"No. Sorry."

"Can you describe her?"

"She's on the younger side. Somewhere between twenty-five and thirty if I had to guess. Attractive. Brown hair, wears reading glasses."

"Anything else you can think of?" Mackenzie asked. "Anything at all."

"I caught a glimpse of her car one time. She'd only been in three times. The second time, I hurried out to the front lobby a few seconds behind her. I watched her leave through the front glass. She hurried across the parking lot and got in her car. An old red one, a sedan, I think."

"Does she schedule her meetings with you?" Ellington asked.

"Nope."

They continued talking, but Mackenzie only heard parts of it. She was still hung up on something Thompson had said. *An old red one, a sedan, I think.*

There had been an older-model red car in Amy Campbell's driveway. A Pontiac. Typically, Mackenzie would call it nothing more than a coincidence. But Amy had been acting strange—scared and suspicious. It was certainly worth paying her another visit.

"Mr. Thompson, thank you very much for your time," Mackenzie said. "We'll let the IDs slide, but you have to stop making them."

"You said a girl is dead, right? And she had one of my IDs?"

"It seems that way."

"Then I'm done. There's no amount of money worth getting involved in something like that."

Mackenzie and Ellington made their way to his door. Ellington gave Thompson one of his business cards with instructions to contact them if he saw that woman again or if she tried to get in touch with him somehow. They left him looking slightly upset, perhaps mulling over the fact that the only item on the dead woman had been one of the fake IDs he'd made.

"So what did you realize?" Ellington said as they hurried back to their car. "You ended the conversation quickly and had that look on your face."

"What look?"

"The one you have on your face right now—like a kid that has just spotted one more present hiding away under the Christmas tree."

"His description of the car. An older red sedan. There was one parked in the driveway of one of the houses I visited. Amy Campbell … and she was nervous. Very suspicious and didn't even hint at inviting me in."

"Looks like we might have our first lead."

"Maybe," Mackenzie said.

It felt right, but given the nature of the case and the way Amy had been behaving, she thought they might need to take a few extra precautions to make sure it wasn't just a coincidence. She hated to waste time in such a way, but in the back of her head she also reminded herself that there was a chance the Community could be involved.

Though she had never experienced it herself, she had read case studies and reports of other cases where the introduction of a religious group into the case made the entire thing a ticking time bomb. And if she could avoid that, Mackenzie was more than willing to take some extra time-consuming steps.

CHAPTER NINE

They headed back to the Fellsburg police station, where the small bullpen area was alive with officers swapping shifts. It was nearing eight o'clock on a Saturday night, a busy time for any police department, no matter where they were located. Burke was nowhere to be found, so they headed to their workspace near the back of the building. It was tempting to simply find a motel and call it a night, but they both knew they'd have faster access to records and other information while at the station.

The first thing they did was look on the police database for any information on Amy Campbell. Her record was stellar, with not even a single parking ticket. Seeing that there was clearly not going to be any help there, Ellington placed a call to the resource offices in DC, putting in a request for a background check on Amy Campbell of Fellsburg, Utah.

That done, they turned their attention to the mysterious religious commune known as the Community. It wasn't hard to find information on it, as a simple Google search turned up plenty of hits. The only problem was that the multiple hits were all redundant. All they could tell for sure was there was a religious community tucked away in the forests between Fellsburg and the smaller town of Hoyt.

It was believed that there were anywhere between 1,200 and 1,500 people living in the community. They occupied a small tract of land in the woods that consisted of small shack-like dwellings and little foot-path avenues that connected all of the homes, the church, and the other buildings.

"Check this out," Ellington said, tapping at his laptop.

He had gone into the police database and found two photos. One was an aerial view, taken from a low-flying plane. It showed the entire ground of the community. It reminded Mackenzie of what she had seen of Amish or

Mennonite communities. There were a few cornfields on the far right side of the grounds, and a pasture of what she thought were goats (it was hard to tell from the distance) on the other side.

The second picture was black and white, and rather blurry. It had clearly been taken by someone in hiding, having snuck up on the grounds through the forest. The pictures showed two buildings Mackenzie assumed to be homes, and four people: two children and two women. The women were dressed quite plainly in basic dresses, their hair done up in ponytails.

Mackenzie went back to digging up more information on the place, but there wasn't much more to be found. The Community had existed since the late 1970s and had laid low, never showing up in the news outside of a few local headlines. Aside from some likely overzealous religious beliefs, they seemed to be a standard run-of-the mill isolated religious people. The fact that they practiced polygamy made it a little darker, but Mackenzie knew better than to assume it automatically opened them up to closer scrutiny. Agents far more skilled and experienced than her had fallen into that nasty trap.

As she looked for more information on the Community, her cell phone buzzed on the table beside her. She recognized the DC area code, but not the number. "This is Agent White," she answered.

"Agent White, this is Assistant Chief Manning at the Marshals office. We had that photo scanned and looked over. There was an angle from her left side that gave us a pretty good shot. We ran it through the WITSEC database but there was nothing. There's a ninety-nine percent chance your woman wasn't in witness protection."

The disappointment was strong but fleeting. She hadn't been exactly sure it would be a promising search, anyway. But if it had proven true, it would have made the case a lot easier.

"Thanks all the same," Mackenzie said and ended the call. She turned to Ellington and said: "Our mystery woman wasn't enrolled in WITSEC."

"That makes things a bit harder."

Mackenzie nodded and closed the lid of her laptop. She'd read about twenty-five articles on the Community and the information was all starting to repeat. She glanced over at Ellington and said, "There hasn't been a single arrest or public disturbance related to the Community?"

"Not on the police database going back twenty years."

"I wonder if Burke has any stories or even rumors we could go by."

Before they could continue this conversation, her phone buzzed again. This time it was a short little burst—a text rather than a call. She picked it back up and instantly fumed when she saw it was from her mother.

Wasn't sure what was too late for you, the text read. **Can you call?**

"E... I'm going to kill my mother."

"If anyone asks, I did try to talk you out of it. But... when?"

She rolled her eyes at him, letting him know now was not the time to joke around about it. She almost decided to ignore the text; she had enough to worry about as it was. But she knew that if she didn't respond, her mother would keep texting until Mackenzie finally caved. Plus, there was the off chance that she might have a legitimate question about Kevin's needs.

She called her mother, pushing herself away from the table. Even that little amount of distance between work and home made her feel somewhat like a mother herself.

She was not surprised that Patricia White answered the phone right away. When she did, her voice was hushed. Mackenzie could imagine her holed up in Ellington's study or the guest bedroom so Frances would not hear her.

"Thanks for calling," Patricia said.

"Is Kevin okay?"

"Yes."

"Is the apartment still in one piece?"

"Of... of course. Mackenzie—"

"Then what is it now, Mom?"

There was a quiet moment from the other end that was quickly broken by the sound of her mother's hurt. "I don't understand. We had such a great afternoon yesterday. We got along, had a great meal, and I felt like you and I sort of reconnected."

"I did, too. But this is the second time you've called me while I'm trying to work. And I swear, if it's for no other reason than to bitch about something Frances has done..."

"Well, what am I supposed to do? She's undermining every single thing I say or do. And it's bad enough that Kevin prefers her..."

"He prefers her because he's familiar with her. And Mom, are you sure she's undermining you or is she just giving you pointers and suggestions on how to please a kid she knows better than you?"

"Maybe this was a mistake."

"What? Coming to finally meet your grandson?"

"Partly. But not just that. It's just..."

Mackenzie did not feel bad for her mother... not at all. But she also knew that if her mother fell back into the bad decisions and dark places that had defined the last decade or so of her life, there may be no return. So she found herself at odds: did she tell her mother what she needed to hear, or did she pacify her?

As much as Mackenzie hated it, she figured she had to pacify.

"Mom, I'm going to ask you this as a favor. I need you to suck it up and stay there. Hang in there until we get back. And you know what? Don't even do it for me. Do it for Kevin. You want to be familiar to him? Then stick around. Give him a reason to remember you."

There was a nervous chuckle from the other end of the phone. "You're right," she said. "It was stupid of me to fly out here just to give up over something like this and go back to the hotel."

"You said it, not me."

"Sorry I bothered you."

"It's okay... just make sure you try not to call or text unless there's something wrong."

"I will. Goodnight, Mackenzie."

They ended the call and Mackenzie swallowed down several emotions that all seemed to fight for control. There was anger, sadness, and pity. She could not decide on one, so she settled for calm indifference.

"One of them dead yet?" Ellington asked.

"No, not yet." She looked to the table—to the laptops and the police reports—and got to her feet. "Want to get out of here?"

"Sure."

They tidied up the space, bagged up their laptops, and headed for the lobby. On their way out, they were once again interrupted by the buzzing sound of a phone. This time it was Ellington's. He answered as they passed through the front doors and into the parking lot. Mackenzie listened to his half of the conversation, not quite clear on who it was or what was being talked about.

He did not hang up until they were in the car, Mackenzie slipping behind the wheel since Ellington was occupied. When he ended the call, there was a perplexed look on his face as he pocketed his phone.

"I think I know why there was no record on Amy Campbell," he said.

"Why?"

"Because according to everything the bureau threw at the background check, she doesn't seem to exist. There are, of course, numerous Amy Campbells, but none fitting my description. None at all. Just like our mystery lady, Marjorie Hikkum, Amy Campbell doesn't seem to exist."

CHAPTER TEN

Bethany was driving exactly the speed limit. She'd been doing it for weeks now, not wanting to draw unnecessary attention to herself. The police presence in Fellsburg after midnight was pretty much nil, but she didn't see the point in taking any chances. Now, of course, there was more than just the police to worry about. After what happened to Marjorie Hikkum, she couldn't be too careful.

To say she was on high alert was an understatement. She had a little canister of Mace hidden under her driver's seat. Driving through the night, down the same two-lane stretch of road she was pretty sure Marjorie had gone running down four nights before, was eerie. The overactive part of her mind was fully expecting to see Marjorie's ghost standing on the side of the road, flagging her down.

She shook that nonsense way. After all, she had other things to worry about. Marjorie had been killed *on their street.* She had been coming to find her and Amy . . . she had no doubt about that. What if those who had come after her knew about her and Amy, too?

It was a horrifying speculation, but she could not let it deter her. The work they were doing was far too important. They'd known there would be danger when they decided to go this route. If they buckled under those fears now, Bethany wasn't sure she'd ever be able to live with herself. She now had the dead body of Marjorie Hikkum as a reminder of what was at stake.

It was 2:15 in the morning, and she was about fifteen miles away from her home in Plainsview. She took a left, coming off of the two-lane and onto another, better-maintained, two-lane. Even before she could really start accelerating, she could see the ghostlike glow of the gas station through the trees. It stirred feelings of excitement and fear in her; her heart started booming in her chest and her grip on the steering wheel grew tighter. As she came to the turn to enter the parking lot, she realized that she was also holding her breath.

The station itself was closed, but the lights over the three gas pumps as well as the blaring BP sign at the corner of the lot provided more than enough to see the majority of the parking lot. She dimmed her lights and pulled in on the far right side, as far away from the green BP sign as she could get. On that end of the lot, the right side of the building could be seen. There were a few old tires piled up, a single junked car, and an old corroded filling tank the size of a small van.

With her heart feeling like it was trying to jump into her throat, Bethany rolled her window down halfway and whistled. It was a quick, soft sound. It was also the first three notes of "It's a Small World After All."

After a few seconds, a frail figure emerged from behind the old filling tank. In the dimmed headlights, Bethany could see a tangle of blonde hair and a thin shoulder. As the woman stepped out of the shadows and made her way carefully toward the car, more of her came into view. She was thin almost to the point of being waifish and had a face that, though clearly dirty, was the stuff of movies. Even with a look of stark horror on her face, she was pretty.

When the woman saw Bethany through the windshield, she dashed for the car. She started crying instantly, perhaps in happiness. Bethany figured the girl was feeling almost the same as she was—a war between fear and relief waging inside of her.

The girl opened the passenger's side door and practically fell into the seat. For a moment, it looked like she might reach over to hug Bethany but then thought better of it. "Thank you," was all she said as she managed to bring her stifled sobs to a stop.

"Of course. I know you're scared, but you're okay now. I'm here for you."

Even before she was done saying this, she was already backing out of the parking lot. Her mind was still on Marjorie Hikkum and how she had likely thought she was free as well. She'd gotten so close, after all. Just several more houses down and she would have made it ...

But she had to push that away for now. This thin blonde woman was a new girl, a new chance.

"How long?" the woman asked. Bethany guessed her to be about twenty or so, surely no older than twenty-five, but she looked like a frightened little girl in the darkness of the car. "How far away?"

"About twenty minutes."

The woman nodded and stared dead ahead, as if she was expecting some gigantic monster to come stomping through the forests.

They were quiet for a moment as Bethany turned onto the road and headed back toward the home she and Amy shared with another roommate. Really, she wasn't even sure what to say. Yes, there were any number of empty encouraging remarks she could make, but she wouldn't cheapen this woman's situation with them.

But she did feel a responsibility to be *human* for her—to be caring. That was what allowed her to ask the one simple question she could think of.

"Are you okay? Are you... are you hurt?"

"No. I think I got out okay. I think—"

The back end of Bethany's car felt like it exploded. The entire back shuddered, causing the car to skid. There was a thunderous noise which she did not recognize right away. But when she fought to straighten the car out on the road, she understood that she'd heard the bone-jarring noise of metal on metal.

She checked her rearview mirror and saw nothing at first. There was the night, the road, the shadow-strewn shapes of the trees.

But then she saw it. Something coming up fast behind her. And now that she could see the approaching shape, she could hear it, too. An engine, revving up as the shape got louder. All she saw were headlights, which were turned off, and a muted grille. And by the time she made sense if it, the vehicle was colliding with the back of her car again.

The girl beside her shrieked. She leaned forward, gripping the dashboard, as if willing the car to go faster. Of course, this did no such thing. Instead, the vehicle behind them—which Bethany could now see was a larger and older-model truck—seemed to be affixed to them. Bethany tried to speed up but could not distance herself from the truck.

Ahead of her, the intersection came into view. Her heart dropped into her stomach as she realized what this meant. She either had to slow down for the stop, allowing the truck to push her as it pleased, or she would have to speed straight across the intersection and into the waiting trees on the other side of the ditch. Neither option was appealing to her.

In the end, she opted for a bit of both. Beside her, the young woman continued to scream. They were tormented screams, the sort that would leave her throat feeling very sore tomorrow. Bethany let off of the gas and swerved hard to the right. She managed to snake into the opposite lane just a bit, but the truck followed right behind. Its bumper clanged against hers, causing the car to tremble and slide to the right.

Bethany righted it back and then, almost immediately, did the same thing again. The intersection was no more than fifty feet ahead and at the speed she was going—fifty miles per hour—she and her passenger were going to be rattled one way or the other. All of a sudden, that can of Mace under the seat seemed incredibly stupid.

This time when she swerved out into the opposite lane, the driver of the truck seemed to anticipate it. He not only slipped her bumper, but this time, he matched her angle and slammed into her. The car lurched forward and skewed slightly left. The back wheels cried out against the pavement and when she reached the intersection, the car was nearly horizontal across both lanes.

The woman beside her was shrieking now. When the car hit the ditch, went about two feet into the air, and slammed into two large pines on the side of the road, she was still screaming. Bethany could hear it even over the sound of the side windows and windshield being demolished.

Bethany was thrown forward, directly into the steering wheel. Her head went buckling forward but the glass of the windshield was no longer solid, so it did not do much damage. The steering wheel, though—it took the breath from her and she was pretty sure something inside of her snapped. She gasped and began to panic, dimly aware that the woman beside her was still screaming. It was dark and Bethany's world was distorted with pain, but she was pretty sure the woman was trying to open the passenger's side door to get out.

Bethany tried to say no, but forming the word seemed to create some sort of pinching pain deep within her chest.

Not that it mattered. While Bethany looked at the woman, trying to get her attention, a figure filled the shattered shapes within the window. It was too dark and the pain was too immense, so Bethany didn't see what happened, exactly. She heard the young woman let out a sharp cry and then there was a quick, wet sound followed by silence. The woman stopped screaming, and she was no longer fumbling for the door handle. In fact, she was not moving at all.

Bethany leaned over to the left, desperately looking for the can of Mace as the figure on the passenger's side moved toward the hood. For a moment, the shape of the killer was hidden in the trees and that was somehow even more frightening. Her hope was that she could blind the killer, then strike him with her door as she opened it and made her escape. It seemed almost impossible, but what the hell else was she supposed to do?

As she leaned for the little canister, the exploding pain in her chest made her realize that the little scenario she had played out in her head would indeed be impossible. She could barely lean over an inch, much less shove a door against a killer and run down a road . . . the same road Marjorie Hikkum had no doubt run down on the night she died.

When the driver's side door was yanked open from the outside, Bethany screamed. It was a short scream, cut off by the horrific tearing sensation in her chest. She was barely aware of being hauled out of the car, a rough hand taking her shoulder and then the back of her head.

In the end, her last thought was that the pain in her chest likely spared her from the final pain that came when she was assailed against the head. The killer was holding something hard that slammed into her head once, twice, then three times. As the life faded out of her, she was pretty sure there was the feeling of being sliced and stabbed, but by that point, there was too much pain and an approaching darkness, swallowing everything, to really even care.

CHAPTER ELEVEN

The phone was ringing, but it was an odd sound. It sounded muted somehow, far off. Mackenzie opened her eyes and it took her a while to understand why. She was not at home. She was not in her own bed and the phone was not right there, beside her bed like it was in her own bedroom. No, she and Ellington were in some small town in Utah and the phone was sitting on the other side of the room, plugged into one of the room's only two outlets.

The similarity she felt from home was Ellington's naked body next to hers. Their legs were haphazardly intertwined—something she didn't care for but she knew he liked—and her arm was draped partially over his chest.

It took the third ring to truly pull her from her sleep. Ellington came with her and by the time he was sitting up, she was already at the small table that held the TV, the coffeemaker, and her phone.

"This is White," she said, doing a poor job to hide the fact that she had been pulled from sleep. Her brain was still trying to make sense of the time she'd seen on her phone when she had answered it: 4:34.

"Agent White, it's Sheriff Burke. We got two more bodies."

"Two more?"

"Yeah."

Hearing his wife say *two more* at four in the morning was all Ellington needed to hear. Even before getting confirmation from Mackenzie, he was out of bed and getting dressed.

"How recent?"

"Not sure. It couldn't have happened more than an hour and a half ago. I'm out here at the intersection of State Road 14 and Highway 27."

"We'll be there as soon as we can."

She ended the call and followed Ellington's example. They got dressed together, the sleep quickly sliding right off of them.

"Two?" Ellington said.

"Two," she confirmed.

It was the last thing said between them before they left. Two new victims at once told them everything they needed to know: this killer was brave and did not mind making bold moves. And while it might seem like that was a recipe for a sloppy killer, they both knew it also made for the more dangerous and cunning ones as well.

They joined Burke and three other officers twenty-one minutes later. The intersection was blocked off on both sides by patrol cars and flares. The flares looked cartoonishly orange against the darkness of the night and the black of the pavement. The rotating bubble lights from the patrol cars and the flickering of the flares revealed a car that had crashed into the tree line on the right side of Highway 27, directly across from an intersection.

Mackenzie felt a fluttering disappointment. Surely Burke would not have called them in to assist with two victims of a car accident, would he?

As they made their way over to the car, where Burke and one of the other three officers were standing, Mackenzie noted the state of the rear of the car. The bumper was dented and partially hanging off. The area where the trunk could be popped open had also been badly dented, the black paint chipped and cracked. The paint had clearly been struck by something lately.

Burke looked up gravely at them. "Looks like it was hit from behind, doesn't it?" he said.

"I'd agree with that," she said. "I wonder how long ago it happened."

"Well, this one is still bleeding," he said, nodding to the ground.

Mackenzie looked behind him and saw a young woman who had obviously been struck in the head several times. There was also a harsh slash mark high across her chest, just below the neck. Her eyes stared up to the night sky.

And, just like the identity-less Marjorie Hikkum, there was a strip of black tape over her mouth.

As Mackenzie and Ellington stared down at the body, lying just outside of the trees, she could hear the approaching wail of sirens. She knew these were not the sounds of a police car, but likely an ambulance. *No need for that*, she thought.

"Anything on the body?" Mackenzie asked.

"Haven't looked yet," Burke said. "Thought you might want that honor."

Mackenzie wasted no time in taking the duty. It was quick work, though. There was nothing in the woman's pockets other than eighteen dollars in cash. She looked the woman over a bit more before walking to the other side of the car. The other body was partially fallen against the car. Her throat had been slit hard and deep. And, no surprise, there was also a strip of black tape over her mouth.

A search of this woman's pockets turned up absolutely nothing. The clothes showed signs of being well-worn and in need of washing. The same could be said for her hair.

"Who discovered the scene?" Ellington asked as he opened up one of the wrecked car's doors.

"A thirty-year-old local," Burke said. "On his way to Salt Lake City. He had no idea how long ago the accident had occurred. He got out of his truck to help and then saw the bodies and called us."

"Where is he now?" Mackenzie asked.

"Back at the station. He threw up twice, poor bastard. I told him to hang at the station because you two might want to talk to him."

As he explained all of this, Mackenzie and Ellington looked the car over. The inside was mostly clean, with the exception of an empty Dr Pepper bottle on the back floorboard. They checked the center console and dashboard and came up with just a few items. There was an old scratched Bob Dylan CD without a case, some lip gloss, thirty more dollars in cash, and a license.

The license clearly belonged to the woman who had been driving the car—the one currently lying in front of the trees on the driver's side. Her name was Bethany Hollister and she was twenty-two years old. Mackenzie scrutinized the license a bit harder and for just a moment, she felt goosebumps prickling her skin.

"Holy shit."

"What is it?" Ellington asked.

"Not sure . . ."

She took the license out of the car and back to the body of the driver. She compared the two and it was undoubtedly the same woman. However, that was not what had Mackenzie feeling like someone had just walked over her grave.

She now had two certainties blooming in her mind, neither a concrete fact but solid all the same.

First, she was pretty sure the license was a fake—no doubt created by their new friend Todd Thompson.

Second, she had seen this woman earlier in the day. She'd caught the briefest glimpse of her behind Amy Campbell as she passed inconspicuously down the hallway.

"I saw her," Mackenzie said. "Earlier today, I saw her."

"Where?"

"In the house where Amy Campbell lived. The same house where I saw a red sedan."

"That *is* interesting," Ellington said. He quickly caught on to her enthusiasm and excitement. As they walked away from the car, the ambulance arrived, pulling in beside one of the cars that was blocking off the intersection.

"Got something?" Burke called out to them as they headed back for their car.

"Possibly," Mackenzie said. "I know it's early as hell, but we're about to pay someone a visit."

CHAPTER TWELVE

Mackenzie had only knocked on a few doors at such an early hour during her few years with the bureau and it was still a difficult thing to do. When you came knocking at 6:40, you were pretty much letting the people on the other side know that there was some form of bad news waiting for them outside.

What truly surprised Mackenzie was how quickly the door was answered. There was no more than seven seconds between her knock and the rattling of the lock being undone from the other side. When the door was opened, it was pretty much the same as it had been earlier in the day: Amy Campbell stood on the other side, holding the door only slightly open. By the look on her face, it was clear that she had been expecting *someone*, but certainly not the FBI.

"Ms. Campbell, remember me?"

"Yes." Her eyes seemed to wander everywhere at once, from Mackenzie to Ellington, to the empty yard behind them and then back again. Her mouth was starting to lower into a frown. Through it all, Mackenzie could actually see Amy start to understand what had likely happened. Even before Mackenzie could lean into the news that she was pretty sure one of her roommates had been killed, Amy was already there.

"Bethany."

Not a question, just stating the woman's name. Her eyes glistened with tears.

"Bethany Hollister and one other woman. We don't know her name."

Amy's face went blank for a moment as the tears started to spill. She then took a single step back and leaned against the wall as a deep wail came out of her chest.

❧   ❧   ❧

It took about ten minutes for Mackenzie and Ellington to bring Amy back around. In those ten minutes, Mackenzie noted something quite interesting. While there was definitely sorrow and grief in her cries, there was a great deal of anger, too. She would go from leaning on Mackenzie for emotional and physical support to then grabbing a book from the living room coffee table and angrily throwing it against the wall with a shriek of rage.

While Mackenzie handled the last stages of helping to calm Amy back to a rational state of mind where she could, at the very least, have a rational conversation, Ellington helped himself into the kitchen where he set about making Amy a cup of tea. Mackenzie could hear the tea pot starting to whistle as Amy began to get a grip over herself.

"Sorry," she said, her voice hoarse and wet from crying.

"No need to apologize," Mackenzie said. "I hate to be the one to tell you."

"What happened?"

"We don't know the specifics, but it appears that someone struck her from behind right at an intersection. The car crashed into some trees and then Bethany and the other girl were attacked. I'd rather not go into the specifics right now."

Amy nodded, wiping a tear away.

"Do you know who the other girl was?" Mackenzie asked.

"No. Her name was *going* to be Felicia Rodham. I've got her license in my bedroom, waiting for her."

"So . . . you're saying Bethany left here to pick that girl up?"

"Yes."

Ellington entered the room, setting down a cup of tea in front of Amy. The light smell of lavender wafted across the living room as Amy lifted and dunked the bag.

"Amy, I know you're trying to process a lot right now, but I have to tell you that there's a large part of me that feels we need to take you in for questioning."

Amy said nothing to this. She sipped from the tea, looking at Mackenzie and waiting to see what she would say next.

"You own a red Pontiac, right?" Mackenzie asked. "I saw it outside yesterday."

"Yeah, a Sunfire. It's old. Why?"

"Because we now know that a woman driving a red sedan-type car has been paying Todd Thompson at the DMV for fake IDs. According to Thompson, the licenses are for women that are part of a religious commune known as the Community. And you've essentially just admitted that you are the woman who has been buying those licenses. And now, within the span of four days, three women who had or were to have those licenses are dead."

"I knew buying those licenses was illegal. But I had no idea... no idea it would come to this."

"Based on what Mr. Thompson told us, he thinks the licenses might be a means for helping women get out of the Community. Is there any truth to that?"

"Yes."

In that moment, Mackenzie became quite certain that whatever snafu the Salt Lake City branch of the bureau had endured in the past within the area had been with the Community. Their reluctance to deal with them was why she and Ellington had been sent out. She wondered what had gone down to make the local branch so timid about the Community.

"Then instead of taking you in, I'm going to ask that you level with me right here, right now. I know your heart is breaking for your friend right now, but I need some answers."

"You don't know how much danger I can get into," she said. "I mean, you see what they do... to Bethany, to Marjorie."

"We can keep you safe. While we look into this, we can keep you safe. But someone has to take that first brave step. Someone needs to come clean on this. Right now all I have is more than enough reason to take you in. Give me something else to keep that from happening. Help me find this killer, Amy."

Amy was cupping her tea in her hands, the cup trembling a bit. Slowly, Amy started to nod her head. "Yeah. Yes, I can do that. But... I'm sorry. Can he step outside?"

She nodded toward Ellington, who looked puzzled by the request. "Me?"

"Amy, he's my partner *and* my husband. I trust him with my life and swear you can trust him as well."

"No. I'm sorry, but... please just trust me, okay? I'll tell you everything I know, but I'd rather not do it in front of a man."

Mackenzie turned to him and gave him a playful smile. Ellington, though, apparently did not find it all that funny. He shrugged and headed for the door. "Fine," he said. "I guess I'll just hang out in the car."

"Thank you," Amy said and then, after a pause, said: "I'm sorry."

"It's okay," he said as he headed back outside.

When the door was closed behind him, Amy slumped back into the couch. She slurped down most of the tea and took a very deep breath. "If they knew I was about to tell you all of this, they'd kill me, too. Hell, they probably already have plans to do it on their radar."

"People within the Community, you mean?"

"Yeah."

"What do they do there, Amy? Why are these women trying to escape?"

"From any regular perspective, the Community seems like a natural and moral place—albeit deeply seated in religious roots and practices. But they have this aura about them that makes them look innocent. For the most part, everyone leaves them alone. But it's just an *evil* place. And no, I don't think I'm exaggerating by using that word.

"I don't know if you know the history of the place, but what the Community is now is this off-shoot of sorts—a fundamentalist sect that broke off from their primary religion decades ago, sometime in the forties, I think. Now, it's more like a prison. Once you're in, you're *in*. And that goes double for the women."

"They practice polygamy there, right?"

Amy nodded. It was clear that she was still having to dig for the energy to talk, but she was doing an astounding job.

"The women are married off as soon as they turn eighteen. There have even been cases where, if a man wants the girl badly enough, they are forced to marry at sixteen. All of the marriages are arranged and there are some men there that have as many as five wives. Sometimes the marriages are even to family members. But when anyone within the Community says anything negative about these practices, they are ridiculed and beaten. Especially the women. When the women are beaten, it is done in front of everyone—to teach the woman a lesson and let the rest of them see what could happen to them."

"Amy ... were you part of it? Is that how you know?"

"Yes," she said. The word came out like a strangled croak. "I escaped two years ago. I was forced to marry my cousin on the day I turned eighteen. I screamed and fought it the entire time, all the way through the wedding night. No one cared. Not even the other women who had been through the same thing. Maybe that's not true; maybe they cared. Maybe they cared but were just too afraid to speak up. The women there ... they're really no better than slaves. They're beaten, they're raped—sometimes by multiple men if the so-called husband is feeling generous—and are expected to raise the kids to buy into that same system. I mean ... can you imagine being a woman married to someone they didn't want, raped on a regular basis, raising girls to accept that it's just the way of things and raising boys to expect that level of control over a woman?"

A creeping nausea had settled into Mackenzie's stomach at hearing all of this. There was anger, sure, but there was also the built-in skepticism that came with any good agent. She did her best to level both of those sides out as she sat on the other end of Amy's couch.

"How did you manage to escape?" Mackenzie asked.

"I just decided to get brave and try it. I lived in one of the shacks closer to the back of the grounds with my so-called husband. After a year or so of routine, I knew how his nights went. I waited for one of the nights when he snuck a few nips of the bourbon he kept hidden beneath one of the floorboards—alcohol is prohibited, though some of the higher-ranking men do it anyway. After he drank, it was like clockwork. He'd wait until he was buzzed and then come to me. It was always rough after he drank but afterwards, he would pass out. Like, deep snoring, nothing was going to wake him up.

"The moment I heard him snoring, I left the shack and ran to the back of the property. I didn't stop a single time. I had it in my head that it was going to happen—that I was going to escape. From the instant my foot hit the ground outside, I just moved forward fast as I could. At the back of the property, when I came to the gate, I made it all the way to the top before I slipped and fell. But even that didn't stop me. I got right back up and scaled it again. About ten minutes later, I was on the edge of a back road. Half an hour after that, I thumbed a ride to Salt Lake City.

"I lived on the streets for a while, until I got desperate enough to trust law enforcement. At the Community, it's drilled into us that we can't trust anyone on the outside, much less a system of laws created by sacrilegious governments. But I was starving and cold and had no choice. So I took the gamble and went to the police. Right away, it was clear they had heard certain things about the Community and even then, I knew it was a slippery slope. But they took the things I told them—the very same things I just told you—and they spent a year or so trying to build a case. It was pretty hard and it all fell apart in the end. Once the Community started to moan about their religious freedom being attacked, that was it. The cops and the FBI all backed off."

"So there were never any arrests?"

"None. As far as I know, the bureau only paid one visit to the place and never even made it on the grounds. They were too scared to push too hard. I get it, I guess. Attacking what people claim is their religious right could get very messy. But I'm telling you ... it's not religion they practice. It's ritual abuse and slavery. Now, the FBI did offer me witness protection after I came clean, so I've lived relatively safely since then. Until now, I suppose."

"So, if Todd Thompson was telling me the truth, you've been working to help the women that are brave enough to escape. Is that right?"

"I've tried. I worked that deal out with Mr. Thompson so these women could get a head start—so they could avoid the mistakes I made at first. When I got witness protection services, they gave me a social security number, changed my name, and helped me find somewhere to work and live."

"And you think the case you presented fell apart just because of them crying about religious freedom?"

"I think that started it, yes. But I also found out that there are male members of the Community that have their hands in many large businesses. Some of them seem to also have ties, somehow, to politicians in Washington. So the religious freedom bullshit has a preliminary cover, but it also doesn't hurt to have friends in high places."

"So then how did you come to meet with women like Bethany?"

"Bethany escaped, too. She'd been free for about eight months now. I let her stay here, and she hasn't been the first. There are two others that have come to me and then have gone out into the world. One is living in Texas right now, working as an intern at a pharmaceutical company."

"So you're running some sort of underground railroad for women that manage to escape?"

"More or less. But..."

She stopped here and let out a sob that seemed to come out of nowhere. She shook it away, but when she continued to talk, it was through tears.

"...but I failed them. Marjorie, Bethany, and now this new one..."

"You think someone is killing them so they won't be able to tell about the things that happen at the Community?"

"Yes. And Marjorie...she was close. She was *right there*," she said, pointing out her window and to the street beyond. "She almost made it."

"So what about tonight? What was the plan?"

"We got word from a contact within the Community that another girl was leaving."

"You have a contact on the inside?"

"I do. And please forgive me, but there is no way in hell I am giving you her name. I can't risk putting her in that sort of danger."

"How do the other women in the Community even know to go to her?"

"I don't know. I think she seeks them out, actually. Most women are perfectly fine to live there, to have that life. But the ones that are unhappy are easy to spot. Anyway, we arranged a time and a place. Bethany left to pick her up and...I guess someone knew."

"You think the insider working for you is tipping someone else off?"

"I don't know. I hadn't even considered it. But...I suppose it's a possibility. Oh my God...I don't even know what to do now. Did I get them all killed?"

"No. You gave them hope." She knew it sounded cheesy and she hated that she had so openly revealed her true feelings about all that she had heard. But she had to say *something*. If everything she'd just heard was true, this poor young woman had been through hell, and was trying to provide others an escape from it.

"Other than the recent murders, you say there are only two others who have successfully made it out?"

"That I know of. There could be others who left on their own. If so, I never heard about it."

"If you can give me the names of those two, I'll do what I can to have agents check in on them, just to make sure. I'll make sure a local officer or two is set up outside of your house while the case is active as well. If there is someone out there actively killing women that escaped..."

"Yeah, I know. I'll give you names. Just . . . can you promise me one thing?"

"Sure."

"If you end up out there, try talking to the women. The men will do everything they can to keep it from happening, but you have to push. That place is airtight when it comes to keeping their secrets in. I don't know if anyone has ever really pushed hard enough."

"Fortunately," Mackenzie said, "I have a knack for pushing."

Chapter Thirteen

Mackenzie sat in stunned silence for about a minute or so, trying to put it all in place. While she typically would look for holes or cracks in stories like the one she'd just heard, she knew that it had all the markers of being genuine. There were people that Amy was willing to give the names of that could verify the lurid claims she'd made. There would be police officers who had taken her statements when she'd come forward with her story. So for Amy to lie about this would be very foolish.

Everything pointed to her telling the truth. She even had Todd Thompson's illegal activities to back up her story. And perhaps most damning of all was the fact that Mackenzie didn't think anyone on the planet could act out that much grief and horror if it wasn't genuine.

"I can put a scare into them," Mackenzie said. "All I'd need to do is make a few calls and coordinate a raid against the place."

"That was one of the ideas that came up when the first case was started," Amy said. "But when they were planning it, they realized the danger of it. If even one person in the Community managed to get off free after a trial, the potential for danger for the women in the Community would be astronomical."

It was a consequence Mackenzie had considered but, in her absolute disgust over all she had heard, managed to ignore. But hearing this woman who had been there and endured so much made it a bit more real. Of course they could not risk such a thing.

"If it came down to it, do you think we could get the other escaped women to testify?"

"I don't know. But I doubt it. It's just too risky."

This is a mess, Mackenzie thought. Once again, she was reminded of McGrath telling them how the local branch of the bureau had tried their best not to get involved—which was why Mackenzie was here in the first place.

"I wish I could explain it better," Amy said. "I was basically starving, freezing on the street, and damn near out of my mind before I caved and went to the police. That's how scared I was. That's how deep they ensnare you. And even if they did think it might be a good idea to go public, the fact that recently escaped girls are being killed would be enough to silence them. Even after they're out of the Community, the assholes still there are finding a way to make examples out of them. You see that, right?"

She didn't. But the more Mackenzie's anger grew, the more she absolutely *wanted* to see it.

"I understand your concerns," Mackenzie said. "So let's do this for now: call the two women you know of. Make sure they are still okay. Let them know what's going on and that someone at the FBI is going to have someone check in on them. But make sure they do everything they can to live life the exact same they have the past few years. Can you do that for me as soon as possible?"

"Yes, of course. What are you going to do?"

"I'm going to pay a little visit to the Community."

"What if they won't let you in?"

The mere idea of getting any sort of resistance from them set a fire deep down in Mackenzie's stomach. "I don't think that'll be an issue," she said.

The confidence in the statement was perhaps a bit callous, but she meant every word of it.

Ellington sat slack-jawed behind the steering wheel. Mackenzie had just told him everything Amy Campbell had relayed to her. He looked puzzled and slightly disgusted. They still sat in front of Amy's house, not wanting to move before they were both comfortable with what needed to happen next.

About ten seconds after Mackenzie finished retelling the story, Ellington sighed. "If her story is true, how in the hell have they gotten away with it for so long?"

"Using religious freedom as a shield," Mackenzie answered. "Amy says she's also fairly sure that some of the more powerful members have powerful friends."

"And you think they'll just let us come on in and pay a visit if we pull up at eight o'clock in the morning?"

"I think I can be pretty convincing when it comes to things like that."

"You got me there." He chewed on it all a while longer and shook his head. "If she was telling you the truth, she was pretty much acting as a hero. You think every bit of it's true?"

"I'm trying to look past maternal instinct and the fact that I'm a woman, identifying with another woman. But yes, I think she's one hundred percent legit."

"These closed-off communities are nothing new, I suppose," Ellington said. "Under the banner of religious freedom, they feel like they have some sort of immunity—and when you get right down to it, I guess they do. There are supposedly reports on at least seventy similar communities at the bureau. From what I understand, it was a mid-tier topic that got escalated back when everything went down in Waco with David Koresh."

Thoughts of the ATF raid on Waco back in '93 spun through her head. She had been quite young when the event occurred, but she'd seen replays and re-broadcasts of it throughout her life. She didn't think things would get that bad in Fellsburg, Utah, but then again, the mere idea of men treating women in such a way in current times was beyond appalling. If men could behave in such a way, were there *any* limits to their behavior?

"I don't think we have a choice," Mackenzie said. "We have to go pay them a visit."

"You know where it is?"

"No, but I bet Burke does."

As she went to dig out her phone, she was surprised when Ellington's phone started ringing. He grabbed it from his pocket, read the display, and let out a curse. He showed the caller display to Mackenzie.

It was his mother. Right away, Mackenzie wondered what sort of self-sabotaging behavior her mother had experimented with after their call last night. It was rare that Ellington's mother ever called, so Mackenzie was expecting the worst.

"Hey, Mom," Ellington answered. "How are things?"

As she started answering, he placed the call on speaker so Mackenzie could hear, too. "Patricia and I were having breakfast with Kevin and started talking about the work you both do. That led to talking about how we felt the traditional roles of marriage should work and *that* turned into a petty heated argument."

"You two are pretty sad, you know that?" Ellington asked.

"Son, I did all I could. She's actually a rather pleasant woman, but the smallest things seem to set her off."

"Mrs. Ellington," Mackenzie said, "I do apologize for that. Is she there right now? Is she listening in?"

"No, dear. That's what I'm calling. She got really mad over this . . . over this stupid little argument. She gave Kevin a kiss on the cheek and then headed out. Said she was going to go to the airport and get out of here as soon as she could. Now, those are her words, not mine."

Mackenzie held back a curse. She grabbed her cell phone and stepped out of the car, pulling up her mother's number. She wasn't sure if she had ever actually cursed her mother out before, but it was sure as hell about to happen.

The phone rang four times and went to voicemail. Enraged, Mackenzie killed the call and, rather immaturely, tried again. She got the exact same result.

"Bitch," she hissed through her teeth.

When she got back into the car, Ellington was ending the call with his own mother. He looked calmer than he had when she'd gotten out, but then again his mother was at least rational about most things. Yes, she could be overbearing at times but she knew how to function as an adult.

"You okay?" Ellington asked her.

"No," she said. "Is your mother okay to keep Kevin by herself?"

"Yes. She's good for at least three days. If we think the case is going to take any longer than that, I just need to let her know as soon as we can. What about your mother?"

"No clue. She's not answering her phone."

"Do we—"

She shook her head as she looked to her phone again. "I'm not talking about her right now. I have to put that out of my mind. Right now, I'm going to see if Burke can tell us how to get to the Community."

"You think you're in the mood for that sort of thing?"

She only nodded but was thinking: *This is the exact mood I'd like to be in if someone tried to keep me from coming inside or pulling the "religious freedom" bullshit on me.*

She knew it was a dangerous way to think, but quite honestly, it felt good. She thought of the fear in Amy's eyes, then saw the three bodies of the recently murdered young women and anger seemed to be the only appropriate response.

CHAPTER FOURTEEN

"This is Burke."

He had the tone of a man who was wide awake and ready to face the day. It was much preferable to some of the small-town law enforcement Mackenzie had worked with who sounded like there might be some dead animal lodged in their throat when they rolled out of bed in the morning. Of course, she remembered that Burke had already been up for hours.

"It's Agents White and Ellington," Mackenzie said. Her phone was on speaker mode, allowing Ellington to also hear the conversation while he drove. "We've had some pretty interesting developments. We spoke with a woman named Amy Campbell this morning. She was roommates with the young woman we found dead tonight, supposedly named Bethany Hollister. Amy has been doing her best to help women escape a nearby religious commune known as the Community."

"Damn. Not that mess again."

"Seems like it," Mackenzie said. "She says there was a minor investigation that ended up dead-ending. You know anything about that?"

"Yeah, I think that was from two years back. But because she went straight to Salt Lake City, the Fellsburg PD was left out of that loop."

"Our director in Washington sort of hinted that the SLC branch of the FBI might be very hesitant to approach the Community. What do you know about that?"

The morning cheer in Burke's voice was slowly fading with each word that came out. "Yeah, that was four or five years ago. There were some teens that went up to the Community's front gate to do some hell-raising. But when they got there, they realized there's actually something of a guard shack at the front and you can't get in. So they found some other way around through the woods and came to a back gate sort of thing. When they got there, they said they heard this wailing, like someone in pain. They took video with their phones and even though you can't see anything other than the shapes of trees and the fences, you can sure as hell hear what they're talking about. They got pretty good audio of what sounds like a woman being beaten or raped or both."

"And no one was ever arrested?" Ellington asked, amazed.

"The kids brought the video public and after a failed investigation on our part, the bureau was called in due to the sensitive nature of the case. It nearly went to trial, but once the Community people started screaming that their religious liberties were being infringed upon, the government stepped away as quickly as they could. The fact that there were no abused women from the Community stepping forward certainly did not help, either."

"Any other problems come out of there since Amy Campbell tried pressing charges?" Mackenzie asked.

"None that I've heard of." He let out a deep sigh and added: "I suppose that's where you're headed right now?"

"We are."

"Do you need any help?" His tone indicated that sending help was the last thing he wanted to do.

"No. If things are as touchy with this place as you say they are, the last thing we need is for them to feel like they're being ganged up on."

"They'll likely feel that way anyway," Burke said. "At the risk of sounding uncaring, these are the kinds of people that have gotten very good at playing the victim."

Thinking of Amy's story, Mackenzie figured there were all sorts of victims in stories like these. The trick was to find out who was actually being victimized and who was using it as a shield.

"I assume they lead a peaceful life, at least to the rest of the world?" Ellington asked.

"Yeah. Before these two instances we've both discussed, they were a little more flexible about letting outsiders in. I assume you saw the photos in the police records?"

"We did."

"If there are any firearms on the grounds, they're incredibly well hidden. I honestly doubt there are, though. In terms of any sort of threat, I think it comes down to a numbers game."

"There are like seventeen hundred of them, right?"

"I think that's a little inflated. It's likely closer to twelve or thirteen hundred. Still, I'd say that's a hell of a lot of isolated folks that buy into polygamy and female abuse."

"Agreed," Mackenzie said. "Listen, we need the address for this place. Also, while we're headed there, it might be a good idea to park a unit somewhere within sight of Amy Campbell's home. If her story is true, we have to assume the death of her roommate could somehow connect it all. That would make her a very likely target if there is indeed a killer knocking off women."

"I'll send someone out right away. And Agents? Look, I doubt you'll be in any physical danger, but be careful out there. The last thing I'd want to see is the two of you walking into some sort of political trap. Based on what I've seen, these people were scream 'religious freedom' at the first smell of trouble."

While Mackenzie had never worked directly with people like that, she had heard horror stories. So while she was not one hundred percent sure what to expect, she felt she was prepared to deal with it.

"Anything else?" Ellington asked.

"That's all I can think of. I appreciate you going out there. No one around here ever wants to because of the risk."

Very aware that they were heading into what might very well be a time bomb, Mackenzie looked over to Ellington and they gave one another a shrug. It would have been a cute synchronized moment if not for what they were driving toward.

"Anyway," Burke said. "Here's the address I have for the place, though it's really just directions to the dirt road that will carry you there."

Burke gave them instructions, which Mackenzie typed down on her phone. Meanwhile, the morning grew bright around them as the day set itself into place, as if pulling up the best seat for the show.

CHAPTER FIFTEEN

The Community was located exactly eleven miles outside of Fellsburg, a little less than a forty-five-minute drive away from Salt Lake City. Ellington guided the car off of a back road that fed off to a dirt track. The track meandered through a little strip of woodland and then along the edge of a rather beautiful field. The sun had come up a little over an hour ago, but it still did a fantastic job of providing a nice morning view along the field and the bordering forest.

The dirt track went on for about a quarter of a mile before it came to an end. It stopped at a shack that closely resembled the sort of check-in found outside of most parking garages. Only this one looked more accommodating, like a child's rendition of a house. There was only one window along the front of it, and a single door on the side. It was quite clear that no one was manning the station.

A chain-link fence ran across the road, stretching on another thirty feet to the right before it was overtaken by the forest. To the left, it was more of the same. The forest on the other side of the fence opened up in a U shape that gradually allowed more and more room for the Community grounds. It allowed the fence to be something of a forgotten item, hidden away in the forest while the rest of the grounds looked totally free and accommodating.

Mackenzie opened the door and got out. She looked behind them and saw that the back road they had turned off of was out of sight. From somewhere beyond the fence, there was a slight murmur of conversation. She was pretty sure she could hear a goat crying out into the morning as well.

"What are you doing?" Ellington asked.

"I was going to knock."

"What?"

Mackenzie walked to the fence. There was a section right beside the gate that had been cut out and filled in with a rather elaborate door. The door, like the fence, was also a chain-link structure, bolted to the side of the little shack and held in place by two latches that were locked from the inside. The door was about eight feet across, enough room to allow vehicles to pass through comfortably.

She slapped at the chain-link fence as hard as she could. The sound was abrasive and broke the still quiet of the morning. "Hello?" she called out.

She looked to the other side of the fence. The immediate area in front of her was only open grass. Several feet beyond were several flower beds that she assumed served as the entrance. Past that, the ground descended slightly. She could see the sides of a few buildings and the tops of several rows of corn over to the left. Other than that, there was nothing.

Ellington came up behind her as she started to slap at the fence again. It made a loud jangling noise, an almost alien-like clatter.

"You want me to just honk the car horn?" he asked.

He was being funny, but she thought it was a great idea. "Would you?"

He looked at her, a bit surprised. But before there could be a conversation about it, they spotted two people coming up the slight hill. They were both male; one looked to be about forty or so, the other no older than twenty. They looked at Mackenzie and Ellington with a degree of wonder. The twenty-something man even seemed to be smiling.

"Good morning," the older man said as they approached the gate. "Can we help you?"

Both men stopped about five feet away from the gate. It was clear they did not intend to get any closer.

"We'd like to have a word with whoever is in charge," Mackenzie said.

"Is this a prearranged visit?" the older man asked.

"If you're asking if I have an appointment, the answer is no," Mackenzie said. "However, I truly hope you'll allow us inside."

With that, she took out her badge and ID and pressed them against the door. "I'm Agent White, and this is my partner, Agent Ellington. We're with the FBI and would like to come inside the grounds, please."

"For what reason?"

"We simply need to ask those in charge a few questions," Ellington said.

Mackenzie nearly followed up on this but she realized that if this was a culture that treated women like trash, Ellington was going to be their best bet at getting inside. So she took a step back and let Ellington do his thing.

"What is it concerning?" the younger one asked.

Ellington chuckled and stepped closer to the fence. "I know you guys are isolated out here, but surely even you guys know how this works. We're the FBI. The *I* stands for *investigation.* That means we ask the questions, not the other way around."

"We do not let many visit the grounds," the older said.

"I'm aware of that. So here's the deal I'm going to give you, and it's going to be the best one you're going to get. You let us in and talk to some folks and that will be the end of it. We'll get the information we need—just Agent White and I—and then we'll leave. But if you cause problems, we'll be forced to go back, do a ton of paperwork, and come back anyway. And when we come back, we'll probably have one or two ore agents with us, probably a few members of the local PD, as well. And maybe while all that paperwork is being filled out, I'll call a few journalists. Maybe a Salt Lake City news team. So you make the call: just Agent White and myself, or about twenty very interested people, some of whom work for the media."

The older man looked incredibly angry. His jaw was set and it was clear that he was not used to being placed in such a situation. The younger man, however, had likely never experienced something like this. His eyes were wide, probably because he had never heard anyone speak to a member of the Community in such a way. But Mackenzie thought she saw a bit of excitement in those wide eyes as well.

"I am not in the position to make such a decision," the older man said. "Stand by while I ask someone who can."

"Thank you very much," Ellington said. He made a show of backing away and sitting on the hood of the car. "We'll be right here, waiting."

The men turned away quickly, the older one looking over his shoulder a single time as they made their way back down the little hill and toward the Community.

"Well done, Agent Ellington," Mackenzie said. She leaned in and kissed him briefly on the corner of the mouth.

"I can be mean, too."

"Yeah, but it's just an act."

"It worked, didn't it?"

She nodded and sat down beside him. They looked through the gate at the opening to the Community while they waited for someone else to arrive.

Chapter Sixteen

Mackenzie had expected a long wait, so she was rather surprised when a trio of men appeared less than ten minutes later. They came over the little hill in a single-file line and approached the gate. Mackenzie had also expected a long drawn-out conversation, but she was shocked there, as well.

Without saying a word, the man in front of the trio went directly to the gate and disengaged the locks. He pulled the door all the way open, smiling at them as he did so. This man looked to be in his fifties. His hair was mostly white, but he had a rugged and handsome face. The other two who had come with him were the same men that had greeted them earlier.

The leader of the three extended his arm, gesturing Mackenzie and Ellington inside. "Come on in, Agents. I'd love to hear why you're here."

Mackenzie was taken aback, but did not want to let it show. She started stepping forward but then slowed to allow Ellington to lead. She was shocked when the older man offered his hand to be shaken. Ellington took it and the man introduced himself.

"Marshall Cole," he said. "Pleased to meet you."

"Agent Ellington, and this is my partner, Agent White."

"I must admit, this is not the first time some form of law enforcement has come by the Community."

"We're aware of that," Mackenzie said.

"So what can we do for you today?"

"Well, I'm sure you understand that we can't give specifics, as we're in the middle of an ongoing investigation," Ellington said. "What I *can* tell you is that in the midst of this investigation, the Community came up in conversation. And because we are not at all familiar with this place, we thought it best to get a lay of the land, maybe speak to some people."

"I understand completely," Cole said. "But you must be aware that we rarely get visitors. Many of them may not speak to you merely out of a lack of trust."

"I expect nothing more," Ellington said. "For now, do you mind just giving us a look around?"

"Of course!"

Cole did just that, leading them down the little hill and into the Community. The other two men flanked them to either side. The younger one walked a little too close to Mackenzie, but that was fine. She and Ellington worked as a fluid team, communicating on near-psychic levels at times. When Ellington had requested to *have a look around*, that was essentially code for Mackenzie to study everything they passed while he kept Marshall Cole talking. She did exactly this, while also listening to the conversation.

"Let me go ahead and get this out of the way," Ellington said. "I hear you are all polygamists. Is that true?"

"Some of us are, yes."

"And do you marry your relatives?"

"No, not at all," Cole said. He chuckled at the absurdity of it. "That is false, though we are aware that we somehow got that reputation."

"And people mostly leave you alone out here?"

"Mostly. We will, on occasion, get a teenager or two that comes by to yell insults. Fairly recently, we had one come by with a paintball gun. We had to call the police on him when he started firing through the fence."

"Do you know if the shooter was arrested?"

"I have no idea. I simply stood by as the police did their job. After that, whatever happened to the young man is none of my concern."

"So you have a fairly decent relationship with the local PD?"

"For the most part," Cole said. "I'm sure you know, being a good investigator, that we have had a few words here and there with other branches of the law."

Ellington nodded to this as Cole led them deeper into the Community. It was pretty much what Mackenzie had been expecting based on what she had seen in the police photos. It reminded her of African villages she had seen photos of, only more well-kept. This was especially true of the dwellings. She could not see inside any of them, but there was no way they were any larger than two bedrooms and a living area.

"How big are the homes?" Mackenzie asked.

"Big enough," Cole answered.

"Can you be more specific?" Ellington asked.

"One bedroom, one large central area that serves as kitchen, dining room, and den. We have five communal showers near the back of the property, and a series of outhouses on the opposite side."

"How many people live here?" Ellington asked.

"Seventeen hundred."

As they walked along a little dirt strip that separated two rows of dwellings, they started passing by some of the Community members. The men looked at Mackenzie as if she had two heads. The women, on the other hand, would not even look at her. Their eyes were downcast and Mackenzie did not see a trace of a smile on any of their faces. The women were all dressed in basic dresses, some with prints, but most just plain white or light blue. It was almost an Amish-style of dress, only a little more colorful and comfortable.

"Mr. Cole, are you in charge here?" Mackenzie asked.

When he answered, she could tell that he did not like answering questions from a woman. She was not at all ashamed that she enjoyed the feeling.

"I am the Chief Elder, yes."

"How many elders are there?" Ellington asked.

"There are four more under me."

"All men?"

"Yes," he said, answering it as if it were the dumbest question he'd ever heard.

"How young do you allow the women to marry?" Mackenzie asked.

Cole did not answer her. He kept walking as if he had not even heard her. The other two men seemed to draw in closer, building something of a wall around the agents and Elder Cole.

"So here's the deal," Ellington said. "I know you guys are a little primitive in how to treat women, but my partner is one of the most skilled agents there is. So you can either answer her questions, or she can start walking around here and asking questions of the women."

"She can try if she wants," Cole said. "But the women are instructed to never speak to strangers."

"Like children?" Mackenzie asked.

Cole sneered at her. Any act he was putting on that he was cool and collected was quickly dissolving. "No, not like children."

"Do they get spankings and beatings as if they were children?"

"No! That's another lie."

As they walked along, tension growing between them, Mackenzie figured she may as well go ahead and knock the rest of his calm act to the ground. As they passed by two women walking side by side, one with a basket of eggs and corn in her hands, Mackenzie stepped in front of them.

"Good morning, ladies," she said. "I'm Agent White with the FBI, and I was wondering if you might have time to—"

The women lowered their heads so quickly that Mackenzie was surprised she did not hear their jaws bouncing from their chests. They hurried their steps and went to the right, in the direction of yet another row of homes.

"That was very rude," Cole spat.

"I was just trying to speak with them."

"I told you that they are not permitted—"

"Yes, I heard that. It sounded so archaic and ridiculous that I had to see for myself."

"I'm afraid I don't know what to say or show you if you are going to be this rude," Cole said, looking at both of them. "I have no idea what your investigation entails, so I can't be a very effective guide, now can I?"

"All I can tell you is that it has to do with sanitation," Ellington said, thinking quickly. Mackenzie bit back a smile at his cleverness. He was not only ensuring they would get deeper into the Community, but also putting Cole's mind at ease.

"Sanitation?"

"Yes. Being that your people don't partake in the census, we have no idea how many people are here or what the living conditions are like. The Environmental Protection Agency is really cracking down on small off-the-grid communities like this. I just need to see the condition of the showers, the homes, the facilities, and any sewage run-off."

"And they send the FBI for that?"

"Standard practice when there's a religious community involved."

Mackenzie, of course, knew this was a blatant lie. Federal agents would not be sent out for such a task unless something had gone wrong.

"So then what's the case?" Cole asked, still not quite buying it.

"We've found eight so-called religious communes in the past two weeks that had their people living in filthy conditions. On two occasions, we've had to go in and make arrests when the leaders refused to allow access. Looking for places in the Salt Lake City area, the Community naturally came up."

The expression on Cole's face made it clear that he hadn't fully accepted this story. Still, he kept walking and leading them deeper into the Community, and that was more than enough for now. As Mackenzie continued to appreciate the clever ruse Ellington has constructed, she continued to take in the sights of the Community.

There were several breaks among the dwellings. Some were occupied by small flower gardens, others by what looked like small herb gardens; she saw mint and basil, rosemary and lavender. They were all growing quite well, giving Mackenzie the idea that most of the people here were agriculturally skilled. She had no idea what healthy corn was supposed to look like, but she was pretty sure the field all the way to the right of the property was just as lush and perfect as any other she'd ever see.

And it was then, as she was looking at the cornfields, that she saw the opened barn. It was looked to be a typical barn that anyone might see at a farm. But this barn had been stripped on the inside and turned into a garage of sorts. There were nine vehicles in it: two tractors, two ATVs, three cars, and two trucks. The barn (or garage) sat to the right of the first few rows of corn, about thirty feet away from them. A thin dirt trail snaked off from the primary walkway Cole and his two minions were leading them across.

"Is that the only means of transportation for all of these people?" Mackenzie asked.

"Yes," Cole said. "As you might imagine, people don't leave here very often. Most only ever leave the grounds in the event of a medical emergency."

"What about pregnancies?"

"It's all done here. We have some exceptionally skilled midwives on the grounds."

"Do you recall the last time someone had to leave to go the hospital?" Ellington asked.

"Quite recently, actually," Cole said. "A middle-aged woman suffered from a rather large kidney stone two months ago. It had to be blasted with a laser at the hospital, and then there was some healing to be done. She was in the hospital for three days and came back here . . . happily, I might add."

"And how was that paid for?" Ellington asked. "I assume there's no insurance out here, so it's all out of pocket."

"With all due respect, that has nothing to do with sanitation."

Mackenzie chuckled at this. Then, giving no warning at all, she veered off from the group. She headed straight for the barn and the vehicles inside.

"Agent White, where are you going?" Cole asked.

"I'm a sucker for a tractor," she said. "I wanted to see what you're working with over here."

"But you can't—"

Cole stopped here, apparently not sure how to finish what he was about to say. Without turning to look back, Mackenzie noted the little tremor of uncertainty in his voice. It was the first time she'd heard him so clearly bothered by something since they had arrived.

Instantly, both of the men who had been accompanying him followed her. She was aware of them falling in on either side of her. She also noted that several people who had been walking along the path and toward whatever morning duties they had were now stopping to watch.

"I'm going to have to ask you not to go in there," Cole said. He was trying to sound authoritative, but it was a weak attempt.

"Just a quick peek," Mackenzie said.

The two men who had been flanking them sprinted ahead of her. The younger of the two reached the door on the right and started pushing it forward, closing his side of the set of wooden double doors.

"I'm going to need you to leave that open," Mackenzie said.

The man said nothing. He kept shoving the door closed, the bottom barely skirting the dirt beneath it. The other man was now at the other door. As his hand pushed against it, Ellington dashed forward and stood in his way.

"Don't close that door," Ellington said.

The forty-something man looked back at Cole. Mackenzie also looked at him and saw that he looked both pissed off and worried.

"Tell them to step aside," Mackenzie said.

"Please," Cole said to the men. "Close the doors. They do not have permission to go inside."

The forty-something man pushed the door. Ellington reached out his hands and pushed right back. He gave a hard shove to his side of the door, and it swung inward. The door struck the man on the other side hard enough to knock him down. Ellington looked to Mackenzie, his gaze essentially telling her: *"If you've got a play here, take it now before things really get out of control."*

Mackenzie hurried forward. She of course had no interest in the tractors, as she had claimed. Instead, she headed for the three cars and two trucks. Fortunately, they were all parked directly next to one another, distanced from the more rugged vehicles.

"You are trespassing!" Cole yelled at them. Behind him, several other members of the Community started to gather and stare.

"Not quite," she said. "The doors were open."

"And we tried closing them."

Even as he said this, the younger man finished slamming his door shut. As he started for the other one, Ellington stood in his way. His hand went for his Glock, hovering over the butt.

"Don't you touch that fucking door," Ellington said.

As Ellington and the younger man stared each other down, Mackenzie approached the first of the cars. She looked it over, knowing what she was looking for but unable to find it. She started to feel panic sinking in, thinking they had caused this scene for no good reason at all.

"Agent White, I demand that you get out of that barn!" Cole was livid now, storming toward the entrance. Ellington stepped in front of him, his hand still hovering over his weapon.

Mackenzie came to the truck last. Right away, she saw exactly what she was looking for.

"Cole, who does this truck belong to?"

"It is no concern of yours. Again, what does any of this have to do with sanitation?"

"We lied about that," Mackenzie said. "Now ... is this *your* truck?"

Cole did not answer and all of a sudden, there were four sets of eyes on him: Mackenzie, Ellington, and his two followers. There were multiple others as well, watching things unfold from a distance. Their peaceful morning had grown suddenly tense.

"Answer the question," Ellington said, raising his voice.

"Whatever you think you have found—"

"Zip your mouth," Mackenzie said. "You either answer my question or you're going to be arrested."

Ellington turned to her, giving her a quizzical glance. But he saw what she had found almost right away as well. His eyes and jaw set firmly as he slowly removed his sidearm.

The truck's bumper had been dented and a small portion of the grille had been nicked and broken along the bottom.

There were deep flecks of black paint around both—the same shade of black as the car they had stood outside of, investigating the dead bodies of two young women.

"Hands over your head," Ellington said.

"You are infringing on our religious freedom," Cole hissed. "You have no right to even be here and—"

Mackenzie had heard enough. She was well aware that she was breaking several lines of protocol but didn't much care. She approached Cole and grabbed him by the shoulder. She then hauled him toward the garage, essentially man-handling him. Cole did not put up a fight. Instead, he called over his shoulder to everyone watching.

"You are all witnesses to this," he screamed. "I am being physically accosted by federal agents and—"

Mackenzie shoved him hard toward the truck. He stopped himself by placing his hands against the hood. He tried turning to face her, but she shoved him again, his head facing the grille.

"Where's that paint from?" she asked. "The truck is red. That paint on the bumper and the grille is black."

Cole said nothing. He turned slowly and smiled at her. It took everything in her not to punch him.

With the smile still on his face, Cole offered his wrists, held together. His eyes were unblinking as he stared her down. *Go ahead,* that stare seemed to say. *Arrest me.*

Mackenzie grinned right back at him. She spun him around and shoved him down hard against the hood of the truck. She pulled his arms behind his back and cuffed him. She knew there were countless eyes of the Community watching her, but she did not care. She pulled a little harder than she needed to when she cinched the cuffs and then jerked him back to a standing position.

"Marshall Cole, you're under arrest for the suspected murders of at least three women," she said.

And as she spoke, she made sure to say it loud enough so that everyone gathered and watching could hear.

Chapter Seventeen

Amy assumed most normal people met with co-workers and colleagues outside of work in a coffee shop or restaurant. But she did not have that luxury. She had to be careful and, as of about three hours ago, she knew she had to be more careful than ever. The visit from the FBI agents and the tragic news of Bethany and the girl who was meant to be Felicia had her more scared than ever. In fact, she was well aware that her life could end at any moment.

It was why she pulled her car into an empty parking lot on the very edge of the business district in Salt Lake City at nine o'clock. She parked behind an abandoned laundromat, pulling her car in directly beside another car. The moment she brought her car to a stop, the woman in the other car rolled her window down. Amy did the same and for a space of about three seconds, the two women simply looked at one another.

The other woman was named Lilith. That was all Amy knew; she had never known the woman's last name. Lilith was in her late forties but looked much older. Every time Amy had seen her, her hair was pulled back into a tight ponytail. Her thin face showed echoes of a woman who had likely once been quite pretty but she now looked perpetually tired and haunted.

"I know it's stupid to ask," Lilith said, "but are you sure about Bethany and the new girl?"

"Yeah. The FBI showing up so early in the morning sort of makes it very real."

Lilith bowed her head and wept. Amy could see that she was fighting through the emotion. Amy knew what it felt like. There was so much emotion that needed to come out, but at the same time, there wasn't much time to waste. Amy looked away, leaving Lilith to her grief.

"Shit, I'm sorry," Lilith said a minute or so later. "I barely even knew her, but..."

"It's okay," Amy said. "Hardly anyone knew her. She deserves to be mourned by *someone*."

She didn't ask, but she assumed that when she had called Lilith almost immediately after the agents had left her house and asked to meet, Lilith had likely known the kind of news that was coming. They had only ever met in emergency situations, and it had never been at such an early hour.

"Amy," Lilith said, tears still in her eyes and streaming down her face. "You have done so much for these women. I appreciate it and I *know* they do. But this is three women in less than a week. It's getting too dangerous. I hate to say it, but—"

"Then don't."

"—but we really need to stop. We've done as much as we can, but at some point we have to face the facts and admit that we are fighting a war we simply can't win."

"No. I refuse to even think that. If we gave up on this, the Community wins. You understand that, don't you?"

"I do."

"Well, that can't happen. Even if it does kill me in the end, I have to keep that fire to their feet. I have to be that thorn in their side."

"Amy...Marjorie was killed *on your street*. How much longer do you think you can remain a secret? How much longer until you're killed, too?"

"I can ask the same of you, Lilith. You've been risking so much. Even if we stopped right now, there's still a very good chance that someone would find out. So to me, giving up is just not an option."

Lilith nodded, wiping a few of her tears away. "Oh, to be young and still so full of rage and vengeance."

"You still have it in you, too."

"I thought I did. But...God, it's so tempting to just let it all go. To forget about what the Community is all about—what it has done to me. I could live blindly and mostly happy, I think."

"No you couldn't."

Lilith laughed sadly, nodding at the same time. "You're right about that, I suppose. So—at the risk of seeming like a bitch—what do you propose we do?

If we're going to keep at this, we need to change something. It's quite clear that they're on to us."

"We have to act urgently. No more one at a time. If you know there are two or three or however many, we get them all at once. Work in groups."

"In a perfect world, that would be splendid," Lilith said. "But for me, on the inside, that many women all at once is going to be incredibly hard to pull off."

"I don't see any other way. It can't just be one here and one there. If multiples can escape all at once, it could expose them. It could end the Community."

Amy could see the fear in Lilith's eyes but she thought she could also see a ghost of the anger she had mentioned earlier.

"What about your other roommate? Shanda, right?"

"Yes. Shanda is fine. She's still a little battered and wounded. She's only been out for a month. She rarely leaves her room, which makes her just about as safe as any of us."

"So she wouldn't be able to assist?"

"Not yet. I'll try talking to her." Amy paused here and then asked a question that usually broke her heart. But given their new plan, it nearly instilled some hope in her to get it out in the open.

"How many do you know of that want out right now?"

"Seven easily. Maybe as many as ten."

"And you'll call me if you feel it's time?"

"Yes. But for now, I need to get going. I need to get back before anyone realizes I'm gone."

Amy nodded and cranked her car. "Thanks for all you're doing, Lilith."

"Same to you. I think...well, I *dare* to think if we're careful we can free more women within the month. And in the long run, God willing..."

"We'll bring the Community down."

"We can dream," Lilith said.

But with the flicker of tears still in her eyes, it was very hard for Amy to believe she meant it.

CHAPTER EIGHTEEN

What struck Mackenzie as particularly odd was just how comfortable Marshall Cole looked sitting behind the table in the interrogation room. He did not look anxious or scared at all. He looked like he might be sitting in a restaurant, waiting for someone else to join him for a meal. When Mackenzie and Ellington came into the room, the bastard regarded them with a smile.

"Good to see you again, Agents," he said.

"Can't say the same," Mackenzie said. She figured if he was going to play the cool and collected villain, she could play the non-caring hero. She sat down across from him, looking him in his eyes. They were calm and serene, a vibrant gray-blue.

Ellington stood against the wall adjacent from her. He folded his arms and took on the same stoic posture he usually assumed in an interrogation room. "Mr. Cole, do you know why we've brought you here?"

"Well, when you were arresting me, I believe you said something about a series of recent murders. Judging from your excitability upon discovering my truck, I assume you think there is a connection between the deaths and my truck. Is that about right?"

"That's very much right," Mackenzie said. "You might be interested to know that there was black paint on your dented bumper and grill. It just happens to be the same color of a car that was run off the road last night. The driver and passenger—both young women—were brutally killed. But that really doesn't surprise you, does it?"

But maybe it did. Had she seen a flicker of shock and surprise in his eyes?

"So, let me get this straight," Cole said without missing a beat. "You think some stray paint on my old truck pins me to some terrible murder?"

"Given the color of the paint and some information we have recently heard about what you and your cohorts do in that Community of yours, yes, I think it's more than enough reason to have brought you here."

"Ah, and there we go," Cole said. "It took less than two minutes for us to get there."

"Get where, exactly?"

"You admitting that part of your decision to arrest me and bring me here is based on things you've heard about the Community. Please . . . tell me exactly what you've heard."

She nearly fell for it. And he slipped it in there so subtly that it made Mackenzie wonder if he had been planning for this day for a very long time. If so, she couldn't even imagine the number of loopholes and exaggerated stories he had in mind to weasel out of this. She knew that revealing everything she had heard would honestly only give him more weapons and traps to ensnare her.

"I think I'll keep those little nuggets for now," Mackenzie said.

Still standing nonchalantly against the wall, Ellington gave it a try. "Mr. Cole, if someone decides they want out of the Community, can they leave just like that?"

"There is usually an exit interview. We use it to find out what about the Community displeases them and why they are leaving. We then seek feedback and counsel from some of the other elders."

"Do they sign a contract or something like that to promise they won't tell outsiders about what goes on in the Community?" Ellington asked.

"No. That's ridiculous. We do nothing in the Community that we would not want anyone on the outside to know about."

"What about the footage of that woman getting the shit beat out of her?" Mackenzie asked.

Again, that flicker of uncertainty flashed across his eyes. But he shook it off like a flea and, again, managed to smile at her.

"Yes, what about it?" he asked, smugly. "Did that woman ever come forward? Was it ever proven that those were indeed sounds of pain or torment? Maybe it was someone who was very sick. Or perhaps they were sounds of pleasure and ecstasy as she made love with her husband."

"Perhaps," Mackenzie said. "I wonder if she was the only wife to that man or if there were many of them. And if all of them make the same noises."

She hated herself for the low blow but God, it felt good. She even saw Ellington give her a disappointed little frown at the dig.

"Back to that again?" Cole said. "Look, if you're hung up on the polygamy part of it, I can tell you what you want to know. I know some women these days have a very hard time digesting it . . . to the point of getting angry that such a place even exists."

"Look, for right now I'm looking beyond the fact that you and the men in the Community have somehow brainwashed the women that live there. All we're trying to do is find a killer that has taken the lives of three young women in the past four days."

"So shouldn't you be asking me about that instead of making assumptions about the Community?"

"Mr. Cole," Ellington said, speaking up before Mackenzie lost what little cool still remained. "The fact remains that we are looking for someone who ran a black car off the road last night. The truck we saw this morning looked to have hit something black. And being that the black paint wasn't faded, it does indeed look suspicious. So Community aside, let's take it from there. Is that your truck?"

"It belongs to me and the title is in my name, yes. But many people use it."

"What is it used for?"

"Mostly things around the commune. Hauling corn, wood, things like that."

"Is it ever taken out of the Community?"

"Yes, every once in a while."

"How often?"

"Maybe two or three times a month. Usually to pick up supplies in Salt Lake City."

"And when was the last time it was taken out?"

"I don't know the last time," Cole said. "But I could find out for you. It was probably about a week ago."

Mackenzie felt like she had taken a back seat. It was probably for the best. She was very aware that her anger was getting the best of her. And she was also aware that Cole was making sure it happened. He'd told her without actually coming out and saying so that he saw her as totally beneath him and, therefore, not fit to question him, as soon as they had shown up at the Community. So, for now, she figured she'd let Ellington handle the questions.

"If we asked you for your whereabouts for the past week, would you be able to provide proof?"

"That would be easy. I've been inside the Community with the exception of a trip into Hoyt two days ago."

"When did you go into Hoyt?" Ellington asked. "What time?"

"Two or three in the afternoon. I met with one of the markets that buys corn from us."

"And you were on Community grounds every hour of every other day within the past week?"

"Yes."

Mackenzie couldn't stand staying quiet. She made sure she was calm and collected before she spoke again, asking, "Earlier, we asked about what happens when people want to leave. How many have left during the entire time the Community has been thriving?"

"Four. The last one was nearly eight years ago."

"Could you give us their names?"

"No. There is a degree of anonymity when someone leaves. It is usually at their request. They want a new life and don't want people knowing that they were associated with us."

"Don't you find that insulting?" Ellington asked.

"Not at all. I do find it regrettable, though. We don't offer Paradise or Eden, but we offer more than the world outside does. It is always sad to lose someone to the outside world."

"Mr. Cole, has anyone ever left without your permission?" Mackenzie asked. "Has anyone ever escaped?"

This time, when the flicker of unease came, it stayed much longer. When he answered, he did so slowly. This time, it was his turn to watch out for traps as he spoke. So far, she and Ellington had not mentioned the names of the women who had been killed ... even if they *were* fake names. It would be foolish to mention such a thing if they truly suspected him as the killer. But now the ball was at least in the air and it was his turn to return it.

"Yes. There have been several people that have slipped away unaccounted for. I'm sure you know of the most recent one if you are investigating anything between Salt Lake City and Fellsburg. That woman brought people very similar to you into the Community. And try as they might—just like you—they were unable to pin their hate and misunderstandings on us."

"Three women are dead," Mackenzie said. "That's a fact. Not a misunderstanding."

"No, the misunderstanding is that something bad has happened in the area and because no one has immediate answers, they assume that a community of people they simply can't seem to understand clearly had something to do with it. It's easy to blame it on those that stand outside of your social norms. It's nice. It's comfortable. Look . . . I understand it and I don't even fault you. But I can't just be the scapegoat."

"The truck is enough evidence. Your Community has nothing to do with it. We'd have brought in Joe Nobody off the street if his truck had a dent with seemingly fresh black paint on it."

"So then what do you need? Proof? Go ahead. I openly give you permission to ask anyone in the Community where I was last night. Or for the rest of the week for that matter."

"No surprise there that your people would tell us anything you've already instructed them just to save your hide," Mackenzie said. "You know what I wonder? I wonder what sorts of things might come to light if we were to raid the Community. If they knew you were out of the picture and there was no threat of punishment or banishment, what might they tell us? And without any warning that we were coming, what would we find?"

"It's quite cute that you think we've never been threatened with such before," Cole said, as smug as ever. "See, the past has taught us how to deal with people like you." He leaned forward, lowered his voice, and said: "I can make similar threats, you know. I have one hundred people that will testify that you and Mr. Ellington forced your way onto our property and manhandled me when I was wrongfully arrested."

"Well now, that would be a lie," Ellington said.

Cole said nothing. He gave the slightest twitch of his shoulders in what may or may not have been a shrug.

It wasn't necessarily proof that he was guilty—though it did swing things further in that direction as far as Mackenzie was concerned—and it did show her that he had been contemplating scenarios like this for years. In the back of her mind, she could see what might be taking place at the Community right now. It wouldn't surprise her at all if someone was moving the truck, hiding it and the evidence of black paint somewhere out in the woods.

"You may as well tell us what we're going to find if we were to search your Community. Because we *will* have it searched." This was a bluff; she had no idea if it would come to that or if the state would even allow it.

"Try all you want. But how long might it take you to get a warrant for that?"

Mackenzie felt herself losing her temper. There would be no hope of reining it in if she let it out. So she got up and walked toward the door, unable to resist one last comment before she left.

"You're right," she said. "It could take a while. Maybe as long as the twenty-four hours we're allowed to hold you here."

This time it was her turn to give a little grin.

As she and Ellington made their way out, it was Cole who got the last word. And though it landed somewhat flat, it still made Mackenzie uneasy.

"Good day, Agents. I must say, I look forward to seeing you again on the day this all comes back to you. Because, mark my words, you *will* regret this."

CHAPTER NINETEEN

They were back in the car, leaving the station and heading back to Amy Campbell's residence. Mackenzie was staring out the windshield, still doing what she could to get a better grip on her anger. It was an anger unlike any she'd felt toward a suspect before. She'd never felt such a feeling of superiority coming off of a suspect, such disrespect and mockery. Cole did it well, speaking in a way that wasn't deliberately offensive, but came off as condescending all the same.

"Cole really got to you, huh?" Ellington asked.

"I don't know what you're talking about."

"It's okay. I get it. He's not used to dealing with strong-willed women, and you're not accustomed to men treating you like a little schoolgirl. Just... if we speak to him again, let's pull back on the verbal boxing match."

"I know, I know..."

They pulled up in front of Amy's house ten minutes later. As Mackenzie had requested, there was a patrol car sitting in the vicinity—across the street and two houses down. Mackenzie and Ellington both subtly showed their badges on the way up the sidewalk, to which the cop in the driver's seat gave them a thumbs-up.

When Mackenzie knocked, she also verbally announced herself; she figured the young woman would be terrified to answer the door in light of recent events.

"Amy, it's Agents White and Ellington."

The sound of hurried footsteps approached the door and it was opened quickly. Amy ushered them inside, her eyes never leaving the yard or the street. She looked incredibly paranoid, to the point of appearing terrified.

"The cop," Amy said. "Did you ask for him to be there?"

"Yes. Just a security measure."

Amy nodded and gave a quiet "Thanks" as she guided them into the living room. The room felt smaller upon the second visit. Mackenzie assumed it was because this was where Amy had spent the last few hours, pacing and making the air thick with worry.

"I thought you'd want to know that we have arrested Marshall Cole," Mackenzie said.

"What?" The word came out rather high-pitched. Her eyes were wide with alarm and hope, a perplexing combination. She had clearly not been expecting such a result.

"There was a truck parked in a barn in the Community," Ellington said. "There was evidence of a recent collision, along with marks of black paint."

Amy considered all of this for a moment. She started to pace in a very small loop, four steps one way and four steps back. She was wringing her hands and starting to murmur to herself. Mackenzie couldn't help but wonder if Amy was going to need some kind of therapy when this was all over.

"It won't be enough," she said. "He'll find a way out of it."

"Amy, he's in custody right now. We have him for twenty-four hours. That means if we can approach someone else from the Community who might have answers, they could speak to us without Cole's watchful eye over them."

"Nope," Amy said, shaking her head. "They won't do it. I can't even begin to tell you how loyal the people in the Community are. It's like a cult. Even the women who are being abused remain loyal. It's . . . it's sick."

"Even if that's the case, I think we have to try," Mackenzie said. "Look, Amy . . . I know you have someone on the inside, working for you. And that person could be the one we need. That's all we need to figure out what the hell is going on."

"No," Amy said, nearly hissing the word through clenched teeth. "I can't do that."

Amy started to cry. Mackenzie wondered if it the tears were the result of the stress or regret that she had given up this bit of information about working with someone on the inside.

"Amy, this person could help us figure out who the killer is. Even if it isn't Cole, someone working with you on the inside would be an invaluable resource."

"I can't. If she was found out, they'd probably kill her. She's risking her life to help me and these women and—"

"—and there's a killer out there, taking out these women you're helping to free. So yes, it's a life or death situation all the way around."

Amy said nothing, taking the time to digest it all. Mackenzie wasn't sure she'd ever seen so much turmoil and indecision on a person's face before.

"We could set it up like a sting operation," Ellington offered. "Your contact would not be outing Cole or whoever the killer might be at all. If we approach it right and your insider can give just the slightest bit of information, we could potentially catch the killer in the act."

"I'm sorry, but no," Amy said. "I'm sorry, but I'm going to remain firm on this. If any part of what you're describing goes bad, there would be a lot of people that would suffer. You don't know what it's like there . . ."

"You're right," Mackenzie said. "We don't. That's why we're trying to help."

"I'm sorry," Amy said. She spoke in the tone of a little girl that is afraid if disappointing her parents. But there was confidence there, too—a grit that told Mackenzie no matter how hard she pushed, Amy was not going to budge.

"You know, Amy," Mackenzie said, sensing that she was venturing onto risky ground. "We've got you admitting to a few illegal activities. And if we wanted, we could consider your current refusal as a charge of obstructing a case."

She let the threat hang in the air for a moment. Amy looked at her with a scowl that, quite honestly, chilled Mackenzie's blood for a moment. Amy strode over to Mackenzie, making her wonder if the young woman was going to hit her.

She did not strike Mackenzie, though. Instead, Amy offered her wrists. She stared at Mackenzie, then to Ellington and back again. Her gaze was unflinching.

"Go ahead, then. Arrest me. Because I'm not giving you the name."

Mackenzie didn't bother wasting time on furthering the charade. She gently reached out and pushed Amy's arms down. "We aren't going to arrest you. You certainly aren't the killer and if you're refusing to give up the name of your insider, you remain our closest source to the Community. But Amy, please remember . . . our first objective as agents is not to bring down the Community. We're here to find a killer. You understand that, right?"

"Right."

"So if you come across any information that might help that, at the same time, would not out your insider, would you please let us know?"

"Of course."

"And you don't need to worry," Ellington said. "We've spoken with Sheriff Burke. There will be a police presence on your street until all of this is wrapped."

Amy sat down on the couch and sighed. She wiped her tears away and looked earnestly at both of them. "I wish I could be of more help. But there are innocent lives on the line and I just...I don't know what to do."

"I know." Mackenzie sat down next to her and took the young woman's hand. "But you'll be safe now. And Agent Ellington and I won't go anywhere until we find this killer. Just tell us this: do you think your insider might know who the killer is?"

"No. I'm all but certain she's just as clueless as we are."

"Well, if that's the case, you need to make sure she's more careful than ever. At the risk of sounding selfish, she needs to be watching her back. If the killer knew where to find the girls that escaped, they may also know who's helping them. Namely you...and maybe your insider as well."

Amy nodded curtly, so Mackenzie said nothing else. She sat there with Amy as Ellington looked back out the living room window toward the police car across the street. Amy's living room was quiet as Mackenzie tried to be there for her while she calmed down. And in that silence, Mackenzie got an idea that, while maybe a bit dishonest, was going to be their best bet at getting some answers.

CHAPTER TWENTY

The rest of the day was spent of the Fellsburg PD and out at the intersection where the crash and murders had occurred the night before. Crime scene investigators had not come up with anything of note. They were taking samples from the clothes of Bethany Hollister and Felicia Rodham, but they weren't expecting results for several more hours.

The car had been looked over meticulously and it was all but confirmed that the killer had never gone inside it. There was nothing to be found at the crash scene, leaving Mackenzie and Ellington to dig deeper into the scant bit of information the police department had on the Community. Sadly, there was more to be found online, though it was tricky to determine which articles were legitimate and factual.

Mackenzie still held firm to the plan she had come up with while sitting in Amy's living room. Several times throughout the day, she'd called Burke to get a report from the officer parked in front of Amy's house. The only activity the entire day had been when Amy went outside to check the mail.

During all of this, she and Ellington remained glued to any information they could find on the Community and Marshall Cole. This included having one of the officers in the station work with the city of Fellsburg to get them topographical maps of the area the Community sat on.

By the time dusk arrived, Mackenzie felt like she knew all there was to know about the Community. And, more than that, it was also time to start working on her plan. She'd shared it with Ellington and while he'd had some reservations, he agreed that it was the best shot they had. As they closed up the files and laptops at their little workstation, Ellington leaned over and snuck a quick kiss.

"This could get interesting," he said.

"It could. But maybe it won't. Maybe it'll be a waste of time."

He smirked at her, as if he knew this was not true at all. "Okay," he said. "Then let's get to it."

Mackenzie picked up her cell phone and placed a call to Sheriff Burke. When he answered, she wasted no time and got right to the point.

"Sheriff Burke, I need you to pull the officer you have stationed at Amy's house. We're going to try something a little different."

Mackenzie was driving an unmarked police car down one of the back roads that led out to the Community. Night had officially fallen, so she had to take the roads carefully. These small rural back roads were tricky when night fell; if you didn't know them like the back of your hand, you had to keep your speed to a minimum.

She had, however, taken scans of the topographical maps and knew exactly what she was looking for. When she came to the gravel road on the right that would then take her to the dirt track that led to the Community's gate, she came to a stop. She double-checked the map, noting a spot that had been circled by one of the other officers. It would be the closest she could get to the Community without being seen—a pull-over spot used by police and the occasional hunter during deer season. She'd still be about a mile away from the Community, but that was fine. At that point in the road, anyone leaving the Community would have to pass by her, as there were no alternate roads leading out.

Mackenzie dimmed her lights as a precaution. There was plenty of land and trees separating her from the gate, but she didn't want to take the chance. She crept along the gravel road and nearly missed the pull-over spot. It was shrouded in shadow and night, a half-circle strip of mostly dead grass off to the left of the gravel road. She pulled in, backed up, and situated herself to that she could see the gravel road from an angle, and killed the engine. She was parked far enough to the right side of the little clearing so that she was well-hidden. If someone saw her, it would be because they were making a point to find someone out there.

It was 9:50 by the time she was settled and staring out into the night. It was a lonely feeling, totally isolated and in the dark. It was actually borderline creepy, especially knowing the sort of people who lived in a gated community a little less than a mile to the east.

She called up Ellington, leaving the phone in the passenger's seat and tilted toward the console as to hide the glow from the screen. She placed the call on speaker and his thin voice filled the car moments later.

"You there?" he asked.

"I'm here. It's dark and uneventful. You?"

"I've been parked outside of Amy's house for the past hour. The living room light is on and I've seen her walk by the windows twice. Exciting stuff."

"Been a while since I've done anything like this," she said.

"Same here. It's pretty boring. We could have phone sex to liven things up."

"Maybe some other time," she said, snickering.

"How do you think Kevin is holding up?"

"He's probably the most responsible person that has been in our apartment for the last few days."

"Still no word from your mom?" he asked.

"No. And I'm trying to just push that out of my head for now. If I let that bog me down on top of this case, things are going to get nasty."

"Nastier than your interaction with Marshall Cole this morning? Yikes."

"I think I'm done talking to you," she said playfully. "Call me if anything changes. Love you."

"Will do. Love you, too."

Mackenzie was left in the car to stare back out into the darkness. Curious, she put the window down a bit to see if there was anything worth hearing. It was killing her to not walk right up to the fences and do some sneaking around. But that could potentially ruin the entire plan, so she had to resist.

She listened to the night for a moment but heard nothing aside from crickets and a few frogs somewhere in the forest. There were no engines running, no cars sweeping by down the back road below her, no signs of life anywhere. She supposed it made this the perfect sort of location for the Community.

She thought about the kind of people who might find solace out here, under the guidance of a man who found it perfectly fine to have multiple wives and to treat women like lesser objects. She wondered how many wives Cole had and how often they were abused. She thought of his calm cadence, his sense of confidence and authority in the interrogation room, and could see how he'd make a suitable leader for a place like the Community. He was stern and sure of himself, something that would likely be seen as stellar leadership qualities in a cult.

The night wound on as she tried to put the pieces of the case together in her head. As she thought of Cole, Amy, and the victims, thoughts of her mother tried to sweep in to ruin it all, but she stamped those thoughts down before they could disrupt her. She'd deal with that nightmare later. For now, the Community was enough of a nightmare to contend with.

Her phone rang at 12:10, shattering her internal musings and exercises. It was Ellington. She answered right away, her heart starting to beat a little harder.

"Yeah?" she asked.

"Amy is on the move. She just came out of her garage, driving an older-model Honda Accord. I'm going to let her get a little bit ahead of me and then follow."

"Stay on the line with me. Let me know what happens."

"Got it. Okay...she's at the end of the street now, taking a right. And I'm officially tailing her."

"Okay. So if she—"

She stopped here, noticing the slightest of breaks in the darkness all around her. It was light of some kind, getting gradually brighter by the second.

"You okay over there?" Ellington asked.

"Yeah," she said, reaching for the keys but not yet starting the car. "I've got movement here, too. A vehicle, coming down the road away from the Community."

"Is it the first of the night?"

"Yeah. It's been dead quiet out here."

"No way it's a coincidence, then."

"I was thinking the same thing," Mackenzie said.

She watched as the vehicle passed by. It was a standard-looking car; hard to tell the make and model in the dark. It passed by her, not slowing at all. She could not make out a driver or any details of the car aside from the shape of the headlights.

"What's going on now?" Ellington asked.

"A car. It just passed by, heading out the other way. This road is a little bumpy and about half a mile off of the paved road. So I need to give him ample distance."

"Be careful. As for Amy, she's heading north. Going the speed limit, being a studious driver."

Mackenzie waited until the car's taillights were out of sight and then counted to twenty. She cranked the car and pulled out of the little pull-over spot, leaving her headlights off. She accelerated until she came to the small cloud of dust left behind by the car crunching along the gravel. Just ahead, she could see the hint of taillights. Mackenzie slowed down, almost coming to a complete stop. She watched as the car ahead of her took a right turn back out onto the unmarked paved road.

Again, she counted to twenty and ventured ahead. She did not put her headlights on until she came to the end of the gravel road. She then turned right, making sure to keep her distance.

"You said Amy is headed north?" Mackenzie asked.

"Yeah. And still headed that way."

"Okay. This car is headed south."

They let the weight of what that could mean rest between them on the open line. When Mackenzie spotted the red flicker of taillights ahead, she slowed again, making sure to stay out of sight.

"Amy is turning left now," Ellington said. "She's currently on State Road 14. And as I'm sure you know . . ."

"The intersection of State Road 14 and Highway 27 is where Bethany's car was run off the road. And hold on . . . the car ahead of me is turning now. Another back road. Road sign says it's called Harbough Road."

Again, there was silence. This time it lasted for about thirty seconds, broken by Ellington. "If this is heading the way we think, I wonder if we should call Burke."

"Not yet. Right now, we have just one single car that *might* be worth checking out. It's not worth making a scene about."

"Well, maybe we'll get there," Ellington said. "Amy just turned onto Highway 27. I'm about three hundred feet behind her and I don't think she's noticed me. I'm about to turn, and . . . okay, so there's a gas station up on the left. A BP station. And she's turning in."

More silence. Mackenzie kept her eyes on the road ahead of her, making sure she did not announce herself to the car in front of her. As she waited for more information from Ellington, the car in front of her stopped and turned right. Mackenzie hesitated a moment and then continued on. When she reached the area where Harbough Road ended, she saw that the car had turned onto Highway 27.

"My guy just turned onto Highway 27," she announced.

"I'm creeping along," Ellington said. "But she's going to spot me soon enough and . . . holy shit."

"What is it?" Mackenzie asked.

"Another girl. She just popped up from behind some tank or something on the side of the building and she's rushing for Amy's car. I've got . . . I've got to get up there."

"Get to them and hide them! If this car ahead of me is headed that way, make the driver think there's no one there."

"Yeah, got it. Here we go."

And with that, the call was ended.

Mackenzie gripped the steering wheel, peering ahead of her. She knew she could creep up on the car now. Even if she gave herself away and the guy tried to outrun her, she could pull him over and demand to know where he had been going. But she also knew it would be better to catch him in the act. So she kept her distance, always making sure his taillights were barely visible ahead of her.

She stayed at this pace until the car veered off of the road. Mackenzie wasn't sure what he was doing until she saw the faint green glow of the BP station lights coming through the trees on the right.

CHAPTER TWENTY ONE

Ellington gave up trying to be discreet the moment he got off of the phone with Mackenzie. He sped into the BP parking lot, scraping the underside of the car as he did so. Amy Campbell turned toward him right away, a look of absolute terror in her eyes. Beyond her, the other girl, who had already reached Amy's passenger's side door, literally looked like a deer in his headlights.

He slammed the car into park and got out quickly. He saw recognition in Amy's eyes, slowly dissolving the fear.

"Amy, you and your friend get back behind that tank," Ellington said. "I don't have time to explain, but you need to do it *now!*"

"Why are you here?" she asked. Oddly enough, she sounded angry.

Ellington raced toward them, taking Amy by the arm and pulling her to the side of the station, to the storage tank the other girl had been hiding behind. "I just told you I don't have time to explain. But if you listen to me, we might have our killer in custody in the next five minutes."

Amy fought for just a moment but then nodded and started rushing forward with Ellington. She looked back to the other girl and said, "Come on!"

The girl looked terribly confused, maybe even a little traumatized based on the blank look in her eyes, but followed along. Ellington ushered them both to the hiding spot he'd seen the girl come away from, his eyes turned back to the road. He did not see headlights yet, but just faintly, he could hear the hum of an engine in the distance.

Ellington hunkered down behind the tank with the girls and drew his weapon. "Don't make a sound and stay still," he said.

He pressed himself against the side of the old rusted storage tank and waited. Within seconds, a set of headlights washed across the parking lot. Some of the light came within just inches of the tank.

There was a slight screeching of brakes and then the sound of a car door opening. Ellington kept his place behind the tank, gripping his Glock, and waited.

The moment Mackenzie saw the car turn into the parking lot, she floored it. The car seemed to leap along the road, enjoying the speed for only ten seconds or so before she had to hit the brakes to turn into the BP parking lot. The back end fishtailed a bit, but she corrected it right away. As she did, a man got out of the car she had been following. He had a crowbar in his hand and was busy looking back and forth between her car and the other two that were already in the parking lot.

Mackenzie stepped out of the car, drawing her weapon. The man took two steps toward her, raising the crowbar like it was a baseball bat. The man was haggard looking, somewhere in his late forties or early fifties. His shifty eyes could not seem to remain still, looking back and forth between Mackenzie and the road behind her and then to the crowbar in his hands.

"FBI," she said. "I suggest you drop that crowbar and stop walking towards me right now."

The man looked back behind him, as if he'd expected to find something back there.

"Eyes on me," Mackenzie said.

Still, the man looked behind him, nearly turning fully away from Mackenzie.

"I said eyes on me!"

At this, Ellington stood up from behind the tank. His gun was also drawn as he took a step toward the man. "I suggest you do what she says."

The man turned back toward Mackenzie. When he dropped the crowbar and it clattered to the asphalt, Mackenzie thought it looked as if the man might start crying at any moment.

"Hands on your head and very slowly walk towards my car," Mackenzie said.

"Let me explain..."

"You'll have plenty of time to explain," Mackenzie said. "First, come over here with your hands over your head and stand directly against the side of my car."

The man was openly crying now. Still, he did as Mackenzie asked, shuffling over to her car. When he got there, Ellington fell in behind him. "Hands on the hood, then slowly behind your back," he said.

Again, the man did as he was asked. As Ellington slapped a pair of cuffs on him, he asked: "Want to tell me why you're here at this hour?"

"Just driving around," the man said through tears.

"I'm sure you were," Mackenzie said. She then looked at Ellington with a wary look on her face. He shrugged, knowing what that looked meant.

Is it really going to be that easy?

While Ellington escorted the man into the back of Mackenzie's car, Mackenzie walked up to the side of the station. She approached it cautiously, not wanting to scare the girls hiding behind the large oil storage tank.

"Amy, it's Agent White. You can come out."

Amy carefully stepped out of hiding. Her face was filled with confusion and the same peculiar anger Ellington had seen moments before.

"You followed me," Amy said. Her tone was accusing, her face growing more and more angry.

"That's right. Sorry if you feel betrayed, but we had a killer to catch. And, as it turns out, it seems we've done exactly that. *Because* we followed you."

"You don't understand!"

At Amy's yelling, the other girl stepped out of their hiding spot. She looked relieved as she spotted the man who had been wielding the crowbar being placed into the back of Mackenzie's car in handcuffs.

"The killer appears to be caught," Mackenzie said. "Amy, you don't have to be scared anymore."

"You think they'll just stop? You think they'll forget about it and move on?"

"She's right," the other girl said, joining them. "If he's the guy you've been looking for, it won't matter. It'll just keep happening."

"You're from the Community, too?" Mackenzie asked.

"Yeah. Got out tonight."

"How?"

"I was helped b—"

"No," Amy said. "No, don't give them a name."

Extremely confused, Mackenzie had no other choice but to do what came next. She eyed Amy with as much compassion as she could while also trying to keep a steeled expression on her face.

"I want you and this new girl to come with me to the station."

"No, we can't. If—"

"I'm not asking, Amy. You can get in as my passengers or you can get in with handcuffs on, as my prisoners."

Amy didn't even waste time arguing. Had she not been through so much trauma, Mackenzie would have described her behavior as pouting. She practically stormed to the nearest car—which happened to be Ellington's—and got into the back. The other girl did the same. She still look baffled and was essentially doing whatever Amy did.

When the girls were both in the back of Ellington's car, Mackenzie and Ellington shared a look over the roof.

"We good here?" he asked.

"I think so. Amy still doesn't feel safe, but . . . I don't know."

"I can't imagine what she's been through, living in that place. Maybe she'll never feel safe."

"Maybe not," Mackenzie said. "For now, let's get this guy to the station and see if we can find any other way to reassure her."

CHAPTER TWENTY TWO

The suspect had chugged three cups of water in the past five minutes. He was too scared to string a sentence together, so Mackenzie and Ellington gave him some time. As the minutes passed, though, Mackenzie wasn't sure if she would describe his emotional exterior as scared. She wasn't sure what it was, exactly; he seemed to switch back and forth between uncertainty and a weird curiosity.

"You ready to talk yet?" Mackenzie asked.

"There's nothing to say. I was out for a drive."

The man had not had any ID on him, but he'd told them his name was Bob Barton. Mackenzie thought it sounded a little too much like the alias of a Marvel superhero and assumed it was fake.

"Out for a drive, with no ID," Ellington said. "And just happened to pull into a closed gas station parking lot about a minute behind two young women."

"So you understand our suspicions, right?" Mackenzie asked.

"I told you. I was just out for a drive. It was complete happenstance that I pulled into that gas station."

"Why did you?" Ellington asked.

"I was getting tired. I was going to see if there was a drink machine there, maybe get a soda."

"But there was no wallet, no ID, no money on you," Mackenzie pointed out. "So how were you going to pay for that soda?"

When it was clear that Barton was not going to say anything, Mackenzie got to her feet. "Where do you live, Mr. Barton?"

"I don't have to tell you anything. Don't I get to call a lawyer or something?"

"Do you have one?" Mackenzie asked.

"No. But I know my rights."

"Maybe you do," Mackenzie said. "But you should also know that, at this very second, there is another man being held in an interrogation room just a few doors down from this one. We brought him in this morning, and we're allowed to hold him for twenty-four hours. You're going to get that same treatment and then we can talk about your rights. It'll give you more time to figure out if you really want to lie to us. So I'll ask you again … where do you live?"

Barton only shook his head. "Can I have some more water?"

Mackenzie responded by reaching out, taking the Styrofoam cup he had been drinking out of, and crumpling it. She tossed the broken remains on the table and left the room.

Ellington followed her out into the hallway, closing the door behind him. "That was mature," he said.

"Don't care. He's not telling the truth."

"I'd agree with that. However, if he *is* from the Community and they're all as loyal as we're hearing, he may not crack at all. I think we might have more luck in trying to get answers from a recently escaped and somewhat scared young woman."

They both looked to the door directly beside Barton's interrogation room and, without another word, walked to it. The two girls stood inside, looking through the two-way mirror that looked into Barton's room. Barton wasn't able to see them and apparently had no idea why the mirror was there. He wasn't even looking in their direction.

"We don't know that he's going to talk," Mackenzie said.

"He won't," Amy responded. "They're loyal to a fault."

"We're starting to understand that about the Community," Mackenzie said. "But you women are the exception. You wanted out and risked everything to get out. So if there is something going on….something beyond the abuse and neglect that might help us figure out if this man is indeed the killer, we need your help."

Amy and the new girl gave one another a look. Mackenzie was relieved to see that there was hope in the new girl's eyes. She had yet to give them a name, and Amy hadn't told them what her new assumed name would be. For now, she and Ellington were referring to her as Jane Doe.

Amy looked to the new girl. "Do you know him?"

"Not personally, but he looks familiar, yes."

"A member of the Community?"

"Yes."

"I know him, too," Amy said. "His name is supposedly Bob Barton. He was married to Marjorie and Bethany."

"To both of them?" Mackenzie asked, amazed. She was not only amazed that those two young girls had been married to this man, clearly close to fifty, but that this bit of knowledge alone seemed to put the final nail in his coffin. There was now a clear link and a clear identification that he was indeed a member of the Community.

"Want to know what's really sick?" Amy said. "He's also Marjorie's uncle."

"Yeah, that's sick, all right," Ellington said.

"I think it's also pretty clear motive," Mackenzie said. "The question remains, though . . . how did he know the two of you would be there tonight?"

"I have no idea," Amy said.

She seemed to be calming down a bit now. Mackenzie supposed it was because this Jane Doe was safe and with the police. The fate that had come to the last few women who had attempted escape had been avoided.

"I hate to go there," Ellington said, "but we have to at least consider that your friend on the inside might also be a Community informant."

"That's not possible," Amy said. "I trust this woman with my life. She risks so much to try to help these girls get their freedom."

"You mean the freedom that Marjorie, Bethany, and Felicia are now enjoying?" Mackenzie asked. "Forgive me for being so blunt, but this woman's track record for the last few days is pretty miserable."

"You're not getting a name out of me," Amy said.

Mackenzie and Ellington looked at the Jane Doe and she shook her head. "I can't. Amy's right. This woman would not betray us. It has to be someone else . . . someone else who knows."

"And maybe," Ellington said, looking back through the mirror, "we're looking right at him."

Mackenzie looked at him, too. She glared at him with a bit too much malice, but the comment that came out of her mouth felt right. It felt *true*.

"More than that," she said. "It seems like we found our killer."

"That's good for you," Amy said. "But if he was indeed sent out to kill us tonight and he doesn't make it back, the Community will know. And then they'll start asking around, interrogating people. My insider is at risk and they will not rest until I'm killed. I know you found your killer and think you've won, but you haven't. This will never end..."

The next comment out of Mackenzie's mouth felt just as real and true as the previous. Also, it felt pretty good to say it out loud.

"Fuck the Community," she said. "We've got the leader in custody and now we've got this bastard in custody. If I have to, I'll bring the place down one creep at a time."

Chapter Twenty Three

Shanda opened her bedroom door and looked out into the dark hallway. It was 3:17 in the morning and Amy still wasn't back yet. She'd still been awake when Amy had left the house shortly after midnight. Amy had whispered through the bedroom door that she'd be back soon.

But that was three hours ago and Amy was still not here. It wasn't often that Shanda was left alone in the house—and never at night—so the fear that slowly started to creep into her was wholly unfamiliar. Sure, she had been scared before, but this was some new kind of fright. This was fright born of the darkness and the night, of not knowing what might be lurking in the shadows while she was at home alone.

Her brain begged her to go back to her room, but the thought of being confined in there while no one else was in the house was suffocating. Slowly, she flipped on the light switch to the hallway. The light helped ease her fear a bit as she made her way into the kitchen. She poured herself some water from the tap and drank it slowly. She looked at the clock over the microwave, staring at the green digital numbers to make sure she had seen the ones in her room correctly.

These read just two minutes ahead: 3:19.

She was afraid Amy was dead. She knew better than to go ahead and accept this as fact until someone told her. And the fact that two FBI agents had been to the house twice in the last day or so allowed her to rest in the fact that someone *would* tell her if that was the case. She was also aware that a policeman had been stationed outside of the house for most of the day. So maybe Amy wasn't dead, another victim of whoever was killing everyone.

Maybe something else had happened. Maybe she was with the police or the FBI and things were actually going well.

Maybe they would not have to hide anymore.

As for Shanda, she'd been living with Amy for two months now. She'd arrived four days after her nineteenth birthday. She'd wanted to leave the Community earlier than that but had never been able to work up the nerve. The deciding factor was when Mr. Cole had come to her on the night before she was to be married. The man she would be marrying was thirty-eight years old and already had two wives. Just before she was to turn nineteen, he had also selected her. Mr. Cole had visited her the night before the ceremony, as he did all women before they were married. To make sure she was pure, he'd raped her. It was the first time she'd ever had sex.

Shanda escaped the following night, after her new husband had his way with her for several hours. The last time, he'd made his other two wives watch. When she escaped, one of them watched her go and never made a sound. Shanda had waved at her, trying to get her to come with her toward the back section of fence all the way to the eastern corner, but she had only shaken her head.

Shanda thought of that woman as she finished her water. That woman could have been free. But, as some of the other women of the Community had told her, you start to give up after a certain age. It becomes easy and almost routine to give up on yourself, to give up on any hope of a normal life.

She supposed that's why the majority of women who tried to escape were younger. The oldest who had attempted escape had been twenty-seven. She'd been caught trying to leave, though. To make an example of her, she was stripped naked and beaten with sticks in the middle of the Community. Afterward, any man, married or not, that wanted to spend intimate time with her was able to do so without repercussion for forty-eight hours.

After that, women stopped escaping.

Until lately, of course. During the last two weeks, there had been six who had escaped. And then, naturally, three months ago, Shanda had made her escape. She had essentially been living in the back bedroom of Amy's house since then. She'd only come out to go to two doctor's visits and for dinner a few times. Other than that, she mostly stayed in her room. That's why the FBI agents had not seen her when they'd come by.

Shanda looked to the landline phone on the kitchen wall. Amy had a cell phone but didn't like to use it because it could be tracked and traced easily. The only phone they used in the house was the landline. Shanda stared at the phone, willing it to ring, hoping for some good news. She had stopped believing in God after seeing what the men of the Community had done to that twenty-seven-year-old who had not quite managed to escape. But standing there in the kitchen, she thought it might be easy to go crawling back to the religion she had been raised in—to pray that Amy might be all right. That she might come through the front door any minute now.

Apparently, God had not turned His almighty back on her. Within a few minutes of casting a lazy prayer to whoever might be listening, she heard the doorknob rattle from the front of the house. It was a noise she'd heard numerous times before, as Amy's house key often got stuck in the lock and needed to be jiggled to get the job done.

Her heart leaped as she dashed for the front door. She was barely aware that she was chanting Amy's name under her breath like a mantra. She wondered what girl would be with her. She dared to think it might be the woman who had watched her slip away three months before.

Ready to pull Amy inside the house and wrap her arms around her, Shanda unlocked the door and swung it open. She let out Amy's name but stopped short, unable to get the second syllable out.

Amy was not standing at the door, anxious to come in.

It was someone else, a face that honestly made no sense.

"No . . ." Shanda said.

Fear, hot and paralyzing, rushed through her body.

The figure standing in the doorway shoved her through the door, sending Shanda stumbling backward. When she hit the floor, the figure came through the door, and though the face was familiar, the look of disgust and rage on it was not. The figure descended on her with something in their hand

Shanda opened her mouth to scream but it never came out.

Chapter Twenty Four

As the morning wore itself down toward four o'clock, Mackenzie was starting to understand that this case was becoming less about getting Marshall Cole and Bob Barton to come clean on all that they had done and more about getting Amy Campbell to share everything *she* knew. There was a very muddy line between the two. Finding the killer and convicting Cole were two very different things—one of which they had not even been sent to Fellsburg to do. Still, it was starting to look more and more like those things were very closely linked.

Yes, for now Mackenzie thought it was a safe bet that Bob Barton was their killer. If he turned out to not be the man they were after, she'd be shocked. But still, even with Barton and Cole in custody—Cole for just a few more hours—the knowledge that there were women who were living in some deluded form of captivity just several miles away was infuriating.

While Ellington sat in with Barton, trying to get him to speak, Mackenzie was sitting in one of the open offices within the Fellsburg PD with Amy. Jane Doe was currently using a cot in one of the holding cells to get some well-deserved sleep. Amy also looked tired, but she was wired on fear and adrenaline. Mackenzie assumed the poor young woman felt that she needed to be the lighthouse for these women, the sentinel that looked over everyone, and would not allow herself to rest.

"Here's where we currently stand," Mackenzie said. "Cole is in custody, but only for a few more hours. We've got people at forensics currently running tests to ensure the black paint on his truck's bumper is the same paint from Bethany's car. Even if it comes back one hundred percent positive, it may not be enough to put him away. Besides that, when the state police went to take the truck away, it miraculously wasn't there. That's a little tidbit we just got about an hour ago.

This will all ding his reputation for sure, and it will have people looking at the Community a little closer, but we can't guarantee an arrest.

"Then we have Bob Barton, the man that appeared to be coming to bludgeon you with a crowbar. Everything there lines up perfectly, but so far the local PD have not been able to find anything in the car to incriminate him. However, we have my testimony, of following him from the road that leads to the Community. Again, if no arrest can officially be made, there's yet another ding against the Community.

"In other words, all we need to bring this whole miserable place down is someone like you. Someone like you who has seen what it's like on the inside. If you can connect some dots to Barton, Marshall, and the abuse that takes place there—and if you can tie the recently murdered girls to it all—that would be it. We could raid the place, rescue the women, and get a positive ID on a killer. We just need you to step up. You were willing to put your neck on the line and rescue all of these women. Why not go this one extra step?"

Amy's eyes seemed to be wandering, as if trying to locate the right answer somewhere within the office. When she finally spoke, each word came out slowly. It was clear that she had thought about this herself in the past and was wanting to make sure she was not trying to talk herself into it.

"It all sounds great. Yes. But what if, in the middle of all of that, someone like Cole finds out about the women who are planning to escape. He'll kill them. And he'll do it slowly. And no one at the Community will say anything to him or turn him in."

"Do you have a list of women who are actively wanting out?" Mackenzie asked.

"No. I get them one by one from my person on the inside."

"And I assume you still won't give me that name?"

"Sorry . . . no."

"Can you get in touch with her and see if she would provide us with that list? Surely she has to know you're involved with the law by now, right?"

"Yeah. And she might just do that."

"If she did, Agent Ellington and I can go into the Community right away and take them out with us. Cole and his people can try to stop us but if he does, that would give us just cause to launch a raid on the place. And I'm assuming he would not want that."

"Are you sure this will work?"

Before she could answer the question, there was a knock at the door. It opened a second later and Burke poked his head in. He did not look happy.

"Just got word from forensics. The color of paint on Cole's bumper and the car do appear to be the same. But there isn't enough evidence from the bumper to make a conclusive connection. They think what they have is enough to *maybe* make a formal arrest and hold Cole for a while, but it won't stand up in court."

"Any evidence that anyone attempted to scrub the paint away from the bumper?" Ellington asked.

"They checked. There's absolutely nothing. The fact the truck is pretty filthy isn't helping either. The amount of dust and pollen may have actually made the paint harder to analyze. That's what they tell me, anyway."

"Thanks," Mackenzie said flatly.

Burke nodded and left the room again. She did her best to stay focused on the task at hand, getting back to what they had been discussing.

"You think you can get your insider to help? Even in the smallest of ways?"

"If we act quickly, I think so. No matter how loyal these people might be, the fact that Cole has been arrested and we currently have another member in custody as well, it's going to cause uncertainty. It just takes a few people to raise questions before everything will start to slowly unfold."

Amy suddenly sat bolt upright in her chair. She no longer looked tired at all. Instead, she looked nervous and energized. "Oh my God."

"What is it?"

"My roommate. She's going to be freaking out."

"I thought Bethany was your roommate."

"She was. But there's another one. She's ….well, she had a much harder time at the Community than anyone I can think of. I need to call her."

Mackenzie handed Amy her cell phone. As Amy pressed in the numbers, she looked at Mackenzie and asked: "She won't come out of the house, much less drive. Could we go pick her up?"

"Of course."

Mackenzie waited, watching as Amy put the phone to her ear. About ten seconds later, Amy's eyes narrowed and she looked at the phone as if it might explode at any moment. She pressed Redial and tried again.

"She's not answering," Amy said as the phone stated to ring in her ear again. When it got to voicemail, she killed the call and pushed the phone back to Mackenzie.

"What if they...?" Amy said.

"Come on. Let's go check. There's no need to worry for right now, right?"

"She would have answered the phone. Oh my God..."

Mackenzie got up and headed for the door. Amy did the same, following slowly behind and doing her best to stifle her sobs. Heading for the door, Mackenzie sent Ellington a text to let him know where she was headed, not wanting to interrupt any progress he might be making with Barton.

In the back of her head, Mackenzie knew it might not be the best idea to take Amy with her. If the news was indeed bad, there was no telling how Amy might take it. But the alternative would have been to argue with the girl about going with her and that was both time and effort Mackenzie was not prepared to waste at four in the morning.

They left the station together, heading across the parking lot. The early morning hours were quiet and desolate, broken only by Amy's quiet sobs.

They had been on the road for only two minutes—roughly nine minutes from Amy's house—when Amy started to talk. Mackenzie did not ask her or prompt her in any way. The young woman simply started to talk. By the time she got the first sentence out, Mackenzie realized she was venting. It was more or less an impromptu therapy session.

"Shanda got it very bad," Amy said. "A lot of the stuff I endured, she got it just as bad. Maybe worse. You can't even imagine what it's like. It's living in horror every day, but doing it in this environment that is peaceful and quiet. And you never know when the abuse is going to come. Mostly it was at night, yeah, but every now and then it would be in the middle of the day."

She stopped here, gazing out the window as if trying to decide if she should keep going. She did not look in Mackenzie's direction the entire time. It made Mackenzie realize how long all of this had been pent up. It had to be hard to release it all to someone who had never been through it all.

"There was one day when I was sitting on the edge of the cornfield, shucking corn. Women did that sometimes, sitting at the edge of the field while the men worked. It's weird as hell … in some respects they almost cherished women. In the Community, women were not meant to work hard or spend too much time doing work a man would be better suited for. It was usually just cleaning, feeding the livestock, shucking corn, things like that. But this day … one of my husbands decided he needed to get laid. And something had pissed him off earlier in the day—I have no idea what it was. So he came over to me, pushed me out of the chair, hiked my skirt up, and took me. Right there, out in the open. A few men watched it happen and …"

"It's okay," Mackenzie said. "You don't have to …"

But Amy shook her head vehemently. She had to get it out.

"When he was done, I didn't even have time to really recover from the act and the embarrassment before one of my other husbands came to me. It was almost like he had to one-up the one before him. It was rough and it was degrading and when he was done, he just left me there on the ground. One of the other women came over to see if I was okay and when she tried to help me back to my house, her husband came over and slapped her. He yanked her away and left me to sort it all out on my own."

"Amy, how many men were your husband?"

"There were three. Men can share the same wives, but they have to be in agreement. They do this so they can trade women around to sort of keep things fresh."

Mackenzie wanted to know more but she was aware that it would only anger her. And God knew she had enough of that surging through her at the moment. So she kept quiet, letting Amy control the tide of the conversation.

It had come to the end, though, Amy having exorcised the demons she had managed to pull to the surface. It resulted in a very tense silence that lingered in the car until Mackenzie pulled the car to a stop in front of Amy's house. She hadn't yet placed the car into park before Amy was opening the passenger's side door and scrambling out.

Mackenzie parked and did her best to catch up to her. She nearly made it, sprinting up the sidewalk and reaching the porch steps just as Amy reached the front door. But Amy stopped before entering and it took Mackenzie about two seconds to figure out why.

The front door was already open. It was opened only a crack, a little wedge of darkness revealed. Amy reached out to open it, a cry already starting to escape her throat.

Mackenzie pulled her weapon and raced up the stairs. "Amy, wait—"

But Amy pushed the door open. It would not open all the way. There was something on the inside pushed against it, preventing it from opening the entire way.

Mackenzie caught sight of a small hand on the floor. She reached out to take Amy, but Amy had already seen it. She slipped away from Mackenzie's grip and squeezed through the doorway. As Mackenzie followed, Amy fell to the floor and screamed.

"Watch your eyes," Mackenzie said. She reached for the light switch and flipped them on.

The scene was simple, yet brutal. A young woman that Mackenzie assumed to be Shanda was lying on the floor. She was on her back, staring up to the ceiling. She'd been badly beaten about the head. A pool of very fresh blood surrounded it. The death was so fresh that Mackenzie noted the wound on the left side of the girl's head that was still pumping out blood.

"Amy, don't look," Mackenzie said.

She reached down and attempted to pull Amy away. It took some prodding and strength, but the woman eventually came away from her roommate and friend. She let out a choked sob and started to fall in toward Mackenzie. Mackenzie, thinking Amy was coming in for an embrace of comfort, opened her arms.

Instead of an embrace, she received a harsh slap right across her face. It staggered her for a moment and all of her instinct in training nearly had her respond in kind.

"This is *your* fault, too," Amy said.

Mackenzie strongly disagreed but said nothing. She was still reeling from the unexpected slap across her face.

"Because of you, they know about me. They know where I live and now Shanda is dead."

"Amy...they killed a girl right there, out on your street several nights ago before we even got here. Did you ever think the escaped girls are inadvertently leading them here? Or it could be your insider, a woman that—"

Amy reared back and brought another slap forward. This time, Mackenzie caught it with her free hand. She then holstered her weapon and gave Amy's arm a slight twist.

"Hit me again and I *will* arrest you."

"They know where I live! Shanda is dead, you've only helped them find me, and now they know where I live!"

Mackenzie released Amy. She fell to the ground by her dead roommate and started wailing. Mackenzie felt her own heart sagging, her emotions strapping into a roller coaster with broken tracks.

She pulled out her phone and when she called up Ellington, she was surprised to find tears in her eyes. She wiped them away and made sure her voice was ready to speak to him while she waited.

"Everything okay?" he asked in lieu of an actual greeting.

"No. Amy's roommate has been murdered. And it's very recent."

She looked down to Amy and the dead girl. She saw all the blood and started to feel that perhaps Amy was right. Maybe a great deal of this was her fault after all.

CHAPTER TWENTY FIVE

Mackenzie snapped awake at the sound of the door opening.

For a moment, it took her a while to remember where she was. She saw Ellington's face and was confused for a moment when he was not bringing Kevin into the room.

Oh, this isn't my bedroom. This is a spare office in the Fellsburg Police Station.

She had no idea when she had fallen asleep. The last thing she could clearly remember was Amy sobbing hysterically as she and Ellington had brought her in. Currently, she and the Jane Doe were in holding while matters with Marshall Cole and Bob Burton were sorted out. It all came rushing back in a panicked blur.

"Sorry," she told Ellington. "I must have fallen asleep."

"You did. But it was for like ten minutes. I thought you'd want to know that we're just about out of time with Marshall Cole. They've already started prepping the paperwork for his release. I imagine Bob Barton will be out soon after that."

This pissed her off, but she'd known it was coming. "We've got almost twelve more hours with Burton. What the hell happened?"

"Just what we've been warned. Cole or his minions even *mention* religious freedom and you can hear the collective sphincter of the local law enforcement tighten up."

"There's got to be some way ..."

"We're working with the BP management to get security footage from the station. If we can get hard evidence that backs up the report that he had a crowbar and was coming after the girls, we can keep him longer. I don't know what good it will do since he's clearly not the killer. But the manager is already saying that the cameras don't reach that far."

"Amy must have known that," Mackenzie said. "That's why she had Jane Doe hiding on that side of the building. She really didn't want anyone to know what was going on . . ."

"She doesn't trust us, the police . . . ..no one."

"Well, can you blame her?" Mackenzie asked. "A man like Marshall Cole can't be touched. He's about to be released and head back to that violent brothel he calls a home."

Mackenzie checked her watch. It was 7:48. She was hungry but the thought of eating made her feel nauseous. Maybe some coffee would tide her over. Maybe it would wake her up and set her thoughts in order. With Marshall going back, it made things a bit more difficult.

Actually, what made things *very* difficult was the fact that Bob Barton had been in the station, locked in an interrogation room, when Shanda had been murdered. It proved he was not the killer, leaving the question of why he had appeared out of the blue at the BP station with a crowbar in hand.

She got to her feet and left the office with Ellington trailing behind her. Just as she was close enough to the break room to smell the coffee, her phone rang. It wasn't even eight o'clock yet, and seeing McGrath's name in the caller display sent a jolt of worry through her.

Scary, yes, she thought. *But at least it's not one of the grandmothers again . . .*

She answered the call, the worry mingling with her hunger and exhaustion. She felt wretched.

"This is Agent White."

"Agent White, can you please tell me what exactly is taking place down there?"

Based on the curt question and the tone he used, she assumed that he already knew the basics. She wasn't sure how, though. Not unless Burke or some other member of the Fellsburg PD had contacted him with complaints.

"Well, sir, it seems that the little bit of information you sort of side-stepped giving us had to do with a religious community. Every single lead we've had has led us towards them and now we find ourselves with a fourth victim and a cult leader who seems to know his way around every question we can throw at him. Sir, did you know the depth of this group when you sent us down here?"

"With all due respect, Agent White, you are in no position to ask questions. As a matter of fact, I want you to wrap up any loose ends in terms of paperwork and then come home on the next flight out. I'm pulling you and Ellington off of this case."

"You're fucking joking, right?" Mackenzie asked. She didn't realize until the question was out of her mouth exactly what she said. She knew if she had not been so tired and thinking with her right mind, she would have filtered such a comment.

"I highly suggest you watch your tongue with me, Agent White. If you like, I can give you further reprimands when you get back."

"You're right. I'm sorry. We haven't slept in about thirty-two hours. But sir... what did we do to have you pulling us?"

Hearing the question, Ellington gave her an expression that mirrored the brash question she had asked.

"We've had complaints filed," he said. "Two of them."

"From whom?"

"You know I can't give you the names. But I can give you the complaints that were filed."

As she was about to ask for the complaints, she looked ahead of her, toward the bullpen. She saw Marshall Cole sitting at a desk. He was answering an officer's questions and the officer was typing something into a computer. Cole smiled at her and it told her everything she needed to know.

The bastard was about to be released—and about two hours early.

"What complaints?" she asked through gritted teeth.

"Well, the first one was concerning your arrest of the leader of the Community. We have multiple witnesses who live on the grounds who say you were incredibly rough with him. That you basically berated him in front of his people."

"Well, I'm a woman and I dared question him. To him, that's punishable by death apparently."

"Agent White, last warning. Watch your tongue. You're getting a taste of what the FBI up there in Salt Lake City went through. And if you and Ellington make this harder than it has to be, it's going to serve as nothing more than another warning. It will make no law organization ever want to go after them again. So please... do the smart thing."

"Fine. I will go on record, though, as saying that while I may have been a bit more physical than I needed to be with him, there was nothing excessive. Now, what was the other complaint?"

"You made another arrest late last night, correct?"

"Yes, we did. A man trailing a young woman. He nearly assaulted her with a crowbar."

"We have a complaint there as well. We're being told you insulted his people and the Community. There is also some sort of injury. A left wrist sprain, I believe."

"Sir, we barely even touched him..."

"This is bullshit," Ellington said.

"I believe you... more or less," McGrath said. "It's hard to do after the way this conversation started. All the same, I need you two off the case and back home."

"If we do that, what happens to the murder case? There are *four* now, sir. And we're close to getting some answers."

"All the same. The SLC branch can wrap it."

"You know as well as I do how that will end. They'll handle it with kid gloves and—"

"This conversation is over, Agent White. Tidy up what you need to and then get on the first plane home. If I don't get a report that you've arrived home within twelve hours, it's going to be bad news for both of you."

He ended the call there. Mackenzie took a deep breath, doing everything she could not to throw the phone down the hall or to punch the wall directly in front of her.

"He wants us home?" Ellington asked.

"Yes."

She stewed in it for a moment, trying to think of something—of *anything*—she could do in the next twelve hours that would help to nail this case closed. As her mind tried to scrape something together, she sipped on a bitter cup of coffee. She was tired, she was frustrated, and she was starting to not want to battle the anger that was slowly building within her. She felt like a time bomb was ticking away inside of her, with no idea how much time was remaining until the explosion.

As she and Ellington made their way out of the break room, they were approached by a younger-looking cop. He looked bright and fresh, a man who had gotten a solid seven or eight hours of sleep the night before. Mackenzie hated him a bit.

"I wanted you to know we were all rooting for you," the officer said. "When I heard you guys had two of those bastards in, I was sure that was it. But I just heard that Cole is getting out of here. But you know . . . at least you put a scare into them. That's got to count for something, right?"

"Not to the four women that have been killed in the past week," Mackenzie said.

"It's going to be interesting to see how he spins it," the officer said. "That fucker is like a savant when it comes to speaking to people."

"Oh, I'm sure his mindless drones will soak up whatever he has to say," Ellington said.

"Those morons, sure," the officer said. "I'm talking about the reporters and the cameras."

"Who the hell would interview that scumbag?" Mackenzie asked.

The officer looked unsettled for a moment. "Ah crap. You guys didn't know yet, huh?"

"Know *what?*"

"The press is here. They started showing up about an hour ago. There's already two news vans out in the parking lot. Reporters getting makeup and sound-checks."

"How the hell did they know?" Ellington asked.

Another voice answered, this one coming from behind them. They turned around to see Sheriff Burke, looking just as tired and aggravated as they were.

"Because they had someone place a series of calls when everything was going down. Someone to file complaints about the arrests, and then someone to call the media to let them know that their religious freedoms were being trampled. It's what happened when the Salt Lake City bureau tried looking into them a few years back." He sighed here and looked at both of them almost apologetically. "It's about to get really nasty."

"Well, it seems we'll miss the fallout," Mackenzie said. "Our director just called and removed us from the case."

Burke chuckled at this, but there was no humor in it. "Might be for the best. If you get a chance to hear how Cole can spin this sort of thing, you'll want to kill him."

And with that, Burke walked past them. He entered the bullpen and seemed to do everything he could to not look in Marshall Cole's direction.

Mackenzie slowly followed behind him but then veered away and headed for the large picture window in the front of the building. She looked outside and saw a third news van pulling into the parking lot, the news crews coming to capture the tale of how the FBI was against religious freedom while, at the same time, slowly burying the news of four recent murders.

CHAPTER TWENTY SIX

When Marshall Cole came out of the building forty-five minutes later, he looked like a different man. He looked like a prisoner of war having just been freed from some overseas conflict. But as he neared that first news camera, he managed a smile that somehow seemed to speak of perseverance and determination.

Burke and the other officer had been right. The man was good—and he hadn't even spoken a single word. It made Mackenzie want to knock his teeth down his throat. She watched it all unfold as she also followed him out of the building. She stayed out of the way of the cameras and reporters, wanting to make sure she did not look as if she was infringing on his space.

As soon as he smiled, the reporters lurched.

"Mr. Cole, how were you treated?"

"Mr. Cole, why was the FBI visiting the Community in the first place?"

"Mr. Cole, do you feel you've been marginalized during all of this?"

Cole paused and looked around at the four different cameras and three microphones in front of him. He did his best to look perplexed but then held up a hand. As he did, a Fellsburg officer fell in beside him, as if to keep the big bad news people away from him. Cole also pulled off a masterful performance of being shocked by the media presence. But the progression of emotion was too staged to be anything but rehearsed; he went from confused, to bewildered, to accepting. *Oh,* he seemed to say to himself. *The media is here. Well my goodness, I suppose I can't be rude. Might as well answer some of their questions.*

He latched on to the last question that had been asked: *"Mr. Cole, do you feel you've been marginalized during all of this?"*

"Marginalized?" he said. "No. But I would say that I have definitely been personally selected as a target. Look . . . I consider myself an understanding man.

I know there have been a few recent murders in the area and so far, there are no leads of any kind. People get scared. People look for answers. And when you have a group of people in your community that differ from the norm—for instance, myself and the Community—it's easy to find a target for the fear and the worry. I get that.

"But I also must protect myself and the people I share my life and time with. And because of that, I must condemn the actions of the FBI. Yes, I have been here once before and, shame on me, you'd think I'd learned my lesson."

"Mr. Cole," a nearby reporter asked, practically breaking her neck to get closer to him. "Can you tell us exactly what happened?"

"Well, the Community was paid a visit by the FBI yesterday morning. They asked to see the grounds and I allowed it. The agents in question were derogatory from the start so I didn't expect much civility. But when they decided that I was not very forthcoming with answers to the questions they were asking, they saw it appropriate to arrest me. Quite forcibly, I might add. And then, once we were here, it was one comment after another mocking my beliefs and way of life. Which, if I'm being honest, I believe is the only reason they came to pay a visit in the first place."

Mackenzie had to clench her jaw to keep from shouting out. She knew it would get on the news and present another side of this bullshit story, but she also knew that it would only drag this nonsense out further.

"Mr. Cole, can you tell us what the FBI's case is built on?"

"They are operating under the belief that these young girls that are being killed are somehow linked to the Community. I believe they are angling for the case that they are escaped women from the Community. And that, I'm sorry to say, is just foolish. They have no proof and I can all but verify that these unfortunate young women were not former members of the Community."

Keep digging that hole for yourself, Mackenzie thought, still making sure she swallowed down every argument that came to her tongue.

"Will you be pressing charges?" another report asked.

The smile crept onto his mouth for just a moment, and then faltered. Cole looked to the ground and Mackenzie could all but hear the cogs and wheels turning in his head. He was up to something, about to put on a performance.

"I cannot pretend that this does not bother me. But . . . I must admit to you all that I lied. A few moments ago, I lied. I wanted to keep it to myself, to . . ."

And then the bastard started crying. He was very good at it, too. It came naturally and it also made Mackenzie wonder once again if the Community had a series of contingency plans for this sort of thing. Was this a scenario and act that they had long ago planned for? Had Cole been rehearsing this for years, knowing the day would come when he would need to break it out?

The officer who was escorting him took a step toward him. Cole seemed to push the officer away as he wiped a tear away and looked back to the reporters. The tears were real and the emotion looked to be real, too. It even had Mackenzie wondering if perhaps there was something to it all that she had missed. But then he spoke, and she was wondering *much more* than that.

"Mr. Cole, what have you lied about?" This question came from the loudest and perhaps bravest of the reporters.

"The girls . . . one of them was indeed a member of the Community."

The silence from the media was almost sickening. They knew they had hit pay dirt. But Mackenzie hung on his every word, too. He was either about to massively mess up his story or he was going to make things infinitely worse for the police and the FBI.

"Who?"

"Which one?"

They were like birds, pecking in the dirt for a worm.

"There is one girl, not murdered. The police have her in custody right now. They are referring to her as Jane Doe but that is not her name. Her real name is Ruth Cole and she is my daughter."

He then hunched over and wailed.

Mackenzie and Ellington simply looked at one another. It was like they'd just watched a decent movie and had it ruined by an unnecessary twist. Mackenzie actually felt herself starting to walk forward, but Ellington reached out and grabbed her.

"No way," he said. "Let this play out."

It took her a moment to put this all together. But she then realized that even though Cole had just delivered this bomb (one she was ninety-nine percent certain was bullshit) he had no idea that they had Amy in their back pocket. And, if Amy wasn't just stringing her along, perhaps her insider as well.

Cole composed himself but, with tears still in his eyes, he stared directly into one of the cameras. "The police have her in custody, thinking they are saving her. But she is my daughter and I want her to come home. I demand them release her to me!"

That was all Mackenzie could take. The asshole was good, she had to give him that. He had played the sympathy card and then had thrown out a card that would likely have some of those watching siding with him—without knowing the facts, of course.

Mackenzie walked forward and made sure she walked slowly and treated Cole gently. "Mr. Cole, let's head back inside."

"No, I've been released!" He said it very loudly, so every camera could hear him.

Mackenzie leaned in, almost whispering. She made herself aware that there were cameras on her. If she did even one thing wrong, it could help not only truly free this man, but also get her into a heap of trouble with the bureau.

"If you want, I can loudly say that I'll do everything I can to release your daughter right now," she said. "You know how bad that's going to look if you turn it down? Fight that on TV and see what happens."

For a moment, there was pure anger in his eyes. He had not expected such a brazen move, yet here they were. He nodded to her, then did the same to the cameras. He even gave a sincere "Thank you" to a few of the reporters as he allowed Mackenzie and his escort officer to lead him back inside.

There was a murmur of conversation among the reporters and the shuffling sound of reporters hurrying back to their vans and pulling out their cell phones. Mackenzie knew what they were doing; they were making sure they were going to make it known that they were among the first on the story. Because based on the final comment Cole had made, the story had the potential to be huge.

When they were back inside and the doors were closed, it was Ellington who let his temper get the best of him. He approached Cole and led him to the rear hallway. But instead of taking him back to the interrogation room he had previously occupied, Ellington pushed him along to the office he and Mackenzie had been sharing.

On the way down the hallways, Burke had also caught wind of what was going on and started tagging along. He looked to Mackenzie for permission to enter and she gave him a nod. As Burke filed into the office and closed the door behind him, Ellington shoved Cole down into one of the free chairs.

"There's some abuse for you, you pretentious asshole," Ellington said. "Man, you're *good*. I've got to give you that."

"I'm afraid I don't know what you're talking about."

"You could run for President with that kind of act."

"Oh, I would make some *much* needed changes to this country, that's for damned sure."

Mackenzie stepped forward, knowing that if Ellington lost his cool, the case would surely be in danger. He was a patient man at heart but when he did explode, he usually had a very hard time reining it in.

"You prove our Jane Doe is your daughter right now, and I'll call every reporter that was out there and tell them you were wrongly arrested and that we may have taken things too far."

Again, it seemed to not be a course of action that Cole had expected from them. "And how would you like me to prove it?"

"When's her birthday?"

"We don't keep up with birthdays at the Community."

"No traces of birth records at all?"

"None. Sorry."

"Your poker face sucks," Ellington snapped.

"I can tell you where her birthmark is, though."

The flash of anger that rocked through her nearly caused Mackenzie to slap him. Instead of physically hurting him, Mackenzie got down into his face and looked him in his eyes. She was not surprised to find that he was unflinching.

"We came here only looking for a killer," she said. "But before we leave, even if it's not you or someone in the Community, I want you to know that it's now my mission to make sure I bring you down."

"You won't be the first," he said. "Isn't that right, Sheriff Burke? Do they know how badly the Salt Lake City agents were treated when they tried bringing down the Community?" He then got up and stood nose to nose with Ellington, as if daring the agent to shove him again. "Now . . . I've been signed out and am free to go. Hold me any longer and I can make a scene about that as well."

He walked slowly toward the door and turned to give them a little wave as he headed out. "I'll be back for my daughter," he said.

And with that, he closed the door just as politely as you please.

"Charming, isn't he?" Burke said.

"How is he not behind bars yet?" Mackenzie barked.

"You saw how the reporters fawned all over him. He's a walking news story. And he used his religious freedom and a shield. Out here in Utah, that means a lot in case you haven't heard."

"I have to ask, though," Burke said. "And please don't get pissed. But he was here, locked up, when Shanda was murdered. Bob Barton, too. So why are you so determined to nail Cole to the wall?"

"You mean besides the fact that he's a scumbag?"

"Yeah, besides that. Can't arrest him for that."

"All of these girls are connected to the Community," Ellington said, putting some bass into his voice. "Sure, these two aren't the killer, but you don't think they *know* who the killer is? Hell, Cole might even be orchestrating it all."

"Yeah, I figure that's probably what's happening." He left it at this and, by doing so, his silence said everything.

His silence said that while they were busy fuming over Cole—a man who was very clearly not the killer—there was still an active killer out there somewhere. He may be in the Community and he may not. But they sure as hell weren't going to find out if they kept all of their attention focused on Cole.

I bet that was the bastard's plan all along, she thought. *To distract us. And like an idiot, I fell for it.*

Not that it mattered, of course. After all, McGrath had pulled them from the case. The only thing she really should be doing right now was looking for flights back home.

Mackenzie took a deep breath, let out a curse, and left the office. She barely caught a glimpse of Marshall Cole once again exiting the building. Another officer escorted him as the reporters once again fell right in line.

Ellington came up behind her and, for just a moment, put on the husband hat. He placed his hand on her waist from behind and whispered in her ear.

"You okay?"

"No. I don't know the last time a suspect has gotten under my skin so badly. I don't like the loss of control."

"So let it go. We need to be looking for flights home. But we also need to keep in mind that there are now four dead women and a runaway who, from the looks of it, would have been number five if we had not stopped it. So we need to come up with some other ideas while we slowly make our exit."

"You happen to have any?"

"None," he whispered in her ear. He then kissed the nape of her neck and headed back for the office. Before he could get inside, Burke came out. He was on the phone, wrapping up a call. His face looked worried and his voice sounded flat as he said his goodbyes.

"That was the guys looking over the BP footage," he explained. "There's nothing at all on it that helps us. Just some shadows flickering in and out. He says you can see the very edge of one of the cars but he's not even sure if it's yours or Barton's."

"So Barton is as good as free, too?"

"Yes."

"Even though he was wielding a crowbar?" Ellington said.

Burke shrugged "Believe me, I get it. It's frustrating as hell. But what else do you expect us to do?"

Mackenzie nearly recommended that the FBI and the entire body of the state police could grow a pair. That would be a good place to start. But the sad reality of it was that she knew where he was coming from. Religious liberties and freedoms had been an effective shield for far too long, and Marshall Cole and his people seemed to understand that better than anyone she'd ever met.

"I'm very sorry," Burke said.

He went back down the hall. After a while, Ellington followed him. Mackenzie was sure it might seem like a form of abandonment to some, but she loved him for it. He had an uncanny radar for when she needed to be consoled and when she wanted to be left alone. He'd read it dead on this time, sensing that she needed some privacy.

Mackenzie remained in the hallway, just outside the office. She could hear the murmurs of conversation as Ellington and Burke spoke, heading down the hall. It droned away, though, as she did her best to come up with something she might have missed. She'd been so caught up in her hatred of Cole that there was no telling what she might have missed.

Four dead young women.

An abusive religious leader who treated women like nothing more than vessels for the pleasure of the Community's men.

And somehow, she was going to be sent home before seeing it all brought to an end.

It was absolutely unacceptable.

But here she was, being forced away, and there was nothing else she could do.

CHAPTER TWENTY SEVEN

The sense of failure in her heart was so strong that Mackenzie actually felt physically ill as Ellington drove them to the airport two hours later. Just before they left the police station in Fellsburg, Bob Barton had also been released several hours ahead of time. Already, in that one simple act, Mackenzie could see how the Fellsburg PD was moving to do what they could to remedy the damage done with the Community. And if it happened too fast, the entire process of finding the killer would slow and then come to a screeching halt. She was sure the Salt Lake City branch would quietly get involved, but they'd be so timid around Cole and his little cult that they'd be highly ineffective.

"You want me to say it?" Ellington asked.

"Say what?"

"That this really sucks. I'm sure we're thinking the same thing."

"How even if the SLC branch gets back into it, they'd be useless because they're so scared of what happened last time?"

"Yeah, that's where I was. More or less."

"This is screwed up, E. How can they get away with something like this?"

"Maybe they won't. Burke seemed like a pretty strident guy. I don't think he'd just let this go."

"I don't know . . ."

"Look. It sucks to say it, but it's not our problem anymore. So right now, just look ahead to the problem we'll be facing when we get back home. Don't forget we have all the drama with our mothers to look forward to."

"Did you forget that my mother threw in the towel? We only have *your* mother to listen to when we get home."

"But really, isn't that enough?" Ellington joked. "We get an hour-long discussion about Kevin's bowel movements and what we should be feeding him."

"Ah yes. Because we don't know how to raise our own child. Maybe we should pretend like we're *really* interested in her advice. Like we . . ."

She stopped here as something clicked in her head. She even raised her hand slowly, giving Ellington the pointer-finger signal for *wait just a minute.*

He did just that. He knew her well enough to know what was happening. She even chuckled a bit before he asked: "Should I just find somewhere to turn around right now or—"

She hushed him, replaying what she had just said in her mind. *Ah yes. Because we don't know how to raise our own child . . .*

"Yeah, I think maybe you should turn around."

"We need to call McGrath first?"

"Not yet. No. I need to call Amy first."

"Want to fill me in?"

Again, she gave him the pointer finger that now stood for *hush* and *hold on a minute.*

She did not have Amy's number, so she called Burke and asked him for it. She was relieved to hear his reply.

"No need," he said. "She's still here at the station with the Jane Doe. Want me to go get her?"

"Yes, please."

As Burke went to fetch Amy, Mackenzie looked over to Ellington and did her best to explain herself. "What if we were so blinded by the bullshit he spewed to the media that we overlooked something that might actually be true?"

"Which was?"

"What if Jane Doe *is* his daughter? What if he had this wild card planted in his back pocket the whole time, waiting to blow us out of the water?"

"If that's the case, wouldn't she have said something?"

"Not if the people in the Community are as brainwashed as we're hearing. Not if Cole ordered her to never reveal who she was. Maybe her loyalty to him is still so strong that—"

She was interrupted as Amy's voice came on the line. "Hello? Agent White?"

"Yes. Amy, listen to me. I know you're trying to protect everyone and that's admirable. As you know, we've been called off of this case but right now, I'm gambling something and I need you to be truthful. Please."

"Sure."

"What's Jane Doe's name?"

"I honestly don't know her real name. And she won't tell me."

"Do you think it's because she might be Marshall Cole's daughter?"

"No!" But she stopped here for a moment and a heavy sigh filled the line. "I mean, I doubt it. If she is, I never knew it. And my insider never told me."

"Okay, I believe you. Just one more thing. It might sound like an odd question, but just humor me."

"Um, okay . . ."

"When is your birthday?"

"February fifteenth. That's what I decided after I escaped anyway. They don't really do the whole birthday thing at the Community."

Holy shit, she thought.

"Amy, can you please stay there until we get back? Give us maybe forty minutes, okay?"

"Yeah, I can do that."

"And don't let Jane Doe out of your sight."

"Sure. Is everything okay?"

"I don't know. Just hang tight."

Mackenzie ended the call and looked at Ellington. She was sure her facial expression said it all, but she tried to explain herself anyway. "I won't go so far as to say Jane Doe is Cole's daughter, but I'm at least willing to consider it. And if she is, then he's probably going to want her back worse than any of the others that escaped."

"But someone was coming after her with a crowbar. You really think he'd put a hit out on his own daughter?"

"I don't know. Why don't you ponder that while you find somewhere to turn around. In the meantime, I'm going to call McGrath to see if we can get one more day."

"To do what, exactly?"

"I don't know," she answered, already pulling up McGrath's number. "But I'm really counting on Amy having a change of heart and helping out."

When they returned to the police station, Mackenzie noticed right away that Amy looked a little livelier than before. The girl was clearly tired, but there was something in her eyes that made Mackenzie think things might be a little different this time. Mackenzie was pretty sure the spark she saw in Amy's eyes was hope.

They were once again sitting in the office Mackenzie and Ellington had been using. Burke, ever the polite host, brought them both cups of coffee without being asked to do so. Mackenzie gratefully picked hers up and started sipping. She'd lost count of how long she'd gone without sleep, but she knew it was reaching the forty-hour mark.

"Amy, you remember what I asked you on the phone, right? About our nameless friend perhaps being Cole's daughter?"

"Yes. But the more I think about it, the more I don't think it makes sense."

"Oh, we're with you on that. He did, after all, send someone to try to kill her with a crowbar. Or, if it wasn't *him* that sent Bob Barton, I'm sure Cole had to have known about it. The thing I keep coming back to is this: if men are sharing women as wives in the Community, how can they keep track of paternity? What if she truly is his daughter and he's going to use that fact to make this whole case blow up on us?"

"I...I'm sorry. I don't follow."

"Four women dead. Five if we hadn't have stopped Barton, I'm sure. But all it's going to take is for Cole to come back with hard proof that Jane Doe is his daughter. He'll say we abducted her and kept his daughter from him. Pile that onto his crap about wrongful arrests and forcing our way onto Community property, and this case will come to an end. There will be some sort of investigation into these murders, but if it's closely linked to the Community, I can pretty much guarantee you nothing will come of it. There may be arrests here and there for the sake pf productivity, but that'll be it."

"So what do we do?" That liveliness had faded at the possibilities Mackenzie had just laid out.

"I know you won't give us the name of your insider," Mackenzie said. "It makes things hard on us, but I respect it. But what *can* you tell us about her? She may be the only way we get a decent picture of what's currently taking place within the Community."

"I don't know..."

"Amy," Ellington said, "our director gave us one more day to crack this and he did that very hesitantly. This is our last chance to knock this out. Please..."

Amy took a moment to answer, and when she finally did she answered quickly. It almost seemed as if she got the information out fast in an attempt to forget she'd given it up at all.

"Some people call her the First Wife. She's been there from the beginning and some say she's had as many as nine husbands while she was there. She was married to Cole for a while but they sort of ... I don't know ... separated. There's no divorce, as you might imagine. But she and Cole sort of just distanced themselves."

"And this First Wife is the one that is helping you?"

Amy only nodded. She looked sad, as if she had truly betrayed this First Wife by giving up this information.

"Is that title like a position of power?" Mackenzie asked.

"No. She's a woman. She has no power there. But she takes a lot of the girls under her wing. She consoles them and sort of coaches them through how to stay sane through the horrors of the marriages. She's like a mother-figure to a lot of the younger women."

"How does she get in touch with you?"

"She has an old phone." Amy considered this for a moment and then, apparently figuring that she had already said too much, decided it was okay to continue. "I think it's a Blackberry. We aren't exactly allowed to easily contact the outside world. She texts me sometimes to let me know what's going on and when there is a girl who wants out."

"Does she try to coerce them into escaping?" Ellington asked.

"Not at all. She only assists the girls that come to her, wanting a way out. Some women are so brainwashed that they're fine with it. They're taken care of, never have to worry about anything—they just need to deal with the abuse and the polygamy."

"If you were to reach out to her, how soon could she respond?"

"It depends. Sometimes ten minutes. Sometimes two or three hours."

"I assume she can't just leave the Community whenever she wants, can she?" Mackenzie asked.

"Actually, she's one of the few that can. She's sent out on occasion to get the necessary supplies for women. She also helps with the produce markets and setting all of that stuff up."

"How can we talk to her?" Mackenzie asked.

"I can't tell her that I've told you about her. She'll feel betrayed. She'll feel—"

"She'll feel like she's doing her part to make sure no other women are killed," Mackenzie said. "Amy…don't you think this First Wife would want this to come to an end just as badly as you do?"

"Yes."

"If you want," Ellington said, "we can frame it to make it sound like we forced you to give us your phone and we figured out what her number was."

Amy thought about it for a moment and then shook her head. Still, she pulled her phone out of her back pocket. "What should I tell her?"

Mackenzie knew she had to be careful here. She did not want Amy thinking that they did not fully trust her source. And honestly, given everything she'd done to help Amy, Mackenzie *did* trust her. Still, she could not bank on the idea that the woman would be relieved that the FBI was so closely involved. Given the nature of the Community, it might make her shut down rather than become eager to help.

"For now," Mackenzie said, "let's just act as if it's you contacting her. I don't want her spooked. I assume you've met with her outside of the compound?"

"A few times, yes."

"See if you can arrange a meeting. Try to really stress that it needs to happen as soon as possible. Like Agent Ellington said, we don't have much time."

Amy sighed, wiped a tear out of the corner of her right eye, and unlocked her phone. As Mackenzie watched the young woman type in a message to the First Wife, she could not begin to imagine the emotional turmoil this must be putting her through. While Mackenzie knew that she had to work to put her hatred for Marshall Cole on the back burner, she could not deny that the look of absolute brokenness on Amy's face gave her one more reason to detest the man.

CHAPTER TWENTY EIGHT

Mackenzie hated to separate from Ellington with such a short expanse of time to wrap the case, but it just made sense. While she and Amy prepared to head out for a meeting with Lilith, the name Amy had finally given up as belonging to the First Wife, Ellington stayed behind with Jane Doe. They had no idea when Marshall Cole would be returning to cause a scene with the supposed purpose of "claiming" his daughter.

To keep up appearances for as long as possible, Mackenzie insisted that Amy drive her car. Mackenzie sat in the passenger's seat, feeling almost guilty. They'd had to push and push to convince Lilith to come out to meet with Amy. Given Amy's urgency Lilith had finally broken down and relented but made it abundantly clear that it was very risky. Seeming a bit surprised that she was able to leave the Community so soon after receiving the text, she'd returned Amy's text within forty minutes and they arranged a meeting for three hours later.

It was close to one in the afternoon when she and Amy entered into Salt Lake City. Amy worked her way into the downtown area, eventually pulling her car into a parking lot that rested behind a row of older buildings. Most of them looked to have long ago been abandoned; the only one still in business was an old rundown laundromat. When Amy parked behind the row of buildings, Mackenzie could see the steam from the dryers coming out of a back vent.

They arrived six minutes later than the agreed upon time and when Amy saw that Lilith had not already arrived, she instantly grew worried. She nearly opened the door and got out of the car to look around, but seemed to think better of it.

"This would be the fourth time we've met," Amy said. "And she's never been late. She's always been here on time."

"She's just running a few minutes late," Mackenzie assured her. "Everything is going to be okay."

"What if they found out? What if someone killed her?"

Mackenzie said nothing because she could tell from the panic on Amy's face that nothing she said could say would calm her down. The girl was a nervous wreck and for the last few hours, random tears had crept from her eyes. She looked almost has tired as Mackenzie, kept awake only by worry and adrenaline.

Two minutes later, relief washed over Amy's face when another car pulled into the parking lot. It pulled up on Amy's side, the driver not even seeing Mackenzie until she had parked the car and stopped. She instantly reached for the gearshift, but Amy had rolled her window down to speak.

"No, wait," she said. "Lilith, it's gotten bad. Shanda is dead, the police have the newest girl that escaped, and Cole is speaking to the media. The FBI has been called off of the case already."

Lilith hesitated and nodded toward Mackenzie through her opened window. "Who's that?"

"I'm Agent Mackenzie White, with the FBI." Mackenzie showed her badge and ID, holding them up.

"Can I see those?" Lilith asked. It was more like a demand.

It was a strange request, but Mackenzie relented. She gave the badge and ID to Amy, who then handed them through her window to Lilith. The First Wife looked them over and looked back to Mackenzie. She was glad to see something like appreciation in Lilith's face. The woman had a hard face, but the look of brief gratitude lit it up somewhat, if only for a moment.

"Someone knows what you're doing," Mackenzie said. "Someone else in the Community is meeting these girls and killing them. And I was hoping you might be able to tell us who it is."

"I'm incredibly careful when I send messages to Amy," Lilith said. "And when I leave the Community, I stop at the end of the road to make sure no one has followed me out. Believe me...I am very careful. I take my liberties very seriously. I, too, attempted to escape many years ago. But I've been obedient to the point of being dehumanized and was able to gain the trust of the elders again. I can't keep risking my freedoms and the ruse I put in place."

"How do you manage to get out so easily?"

"Well, it was easy this morning because Marshall hadn't returned yet. I left a message with one of his second-in-command, telling them I had a meeting with a woman about the next haul of corn. Marshall never asks questions because he doesn't care. As long as things roll smoothly, he's happy."

Amy spoke next, her voice thick with tears. "Lilith, I'm sorry I told her. I had to, though. All those girls..."

"It's okay," Lilith said, sounding like she legitimately meant it. "You had no choice. And Agent White, I thank you for getting things this far. But the media is involved now and pretty soon, Marshall will get out of it. It's just a fact."

"He's just a bonus, if I can make it happen," Mackenzie said. "For right now, I just want to find the killer. And I've only got about fifteen hours left to get it done."

"So how can I help?"

"Amy tells me you are the original wife of the Community—that you are in fact one of Marshall Cole's wives. But you grew apart, right? Would he still talk intimately with you about things that are going on in the Community?"

"No. He hasn't spoken more than several sentences to me in the past year or so."

"Why not?"

"Many years ago, I tried to speak up for the women. No one dared hurt me or reprimand me because I was Marshall's wife. Some of the girls started coming to me for solace and advice. Marshall saw that as a sign of power and influence...coming from a woman. It disgusts him, and I'm sure he'd love to just kill me or banish me. But that would admit that I hold something over him and he can't admit such a thing, even in such a roundabout way."

"He says the Jane Doe we have in custody right now is named Ruth. Ruth Cole. He says she is his daughter."

"Yes. And mine as well. I've had three children by that wretched man. Ruth was the second. And several months ago, she was assigned to be married to a man thirty years older than her. The things he did to...to *prepare her* for their wedding night pushed her to leave. I took great joy in helping her escape."

"Even when you knew the other girls were being killed as soon as they got out?"

"It sounds terrible, I know. But you can't imagine the terror and absolute sense of worthlessness for the women living in the Community. The chance she had of making it out and avoiding the killer was enough for me. Any chance at freedom . . . of knowing what a normal life could be like. But now that she's out, please . . . do what you can to make sure he doesn't get her back."

"My partner is at the station with her right now to prevent that exact thing."

"Thank you . . ."

She paused here, starting to get choked up.

"And you honestly have no idea who is killing these young women?" Mackenzie asked.

"No. It could be anyone. Marshall has many men beneath him that do his bidding. Bob Barton is one of them. And I would not put it past him to kill someone."

"But he was occupied at the police station when Shanda was killed," Amy said. "It's not him."

"I really have no idea. When I get back I can maybe do some digging. Try to have casual conversations with the men to find out where some of them have been lately . . . find out who has been off the Community grounds. That sort of thing."

"That would be helpful," Mackenzie said. "But again, we don't have much time. I fear once my partner and I are pulled off of this, the case is going to peter out and be forgotten."

"Do you have a plan?"

"That depends. Would you be willing to wear a wire?"

Lilith's eyes grew wide for a moment. She chewed the idea over for a moment but ended up shaking her head. Mackenzie was not all that surprised, but it was still irritating.

"I can't risk that," Lilith said. "It's just too dangerous. You have to understand. If I get found out, he'll have me killed. And then there will be no one left to help these poor girls escape."

"Okay, let's try a second approach then," Mackenzie said. "When we leave here, you come with us. Come back to the police station and tell them everything you know. After you tell it all, we can keep you safe. And if there's enough in what you have to say, we can get the authority to raid the Community."

"You don't think I've thought of that before? That I haven't fantasized about it, even? But do you know it comes down to in the end? It comes down to a middle-aged woman sounding angry and depressed because she made the choice to be involved in a group like that. It will be my word against almost everyone else's in the Community. My life would be over, even if I did manage to pick up the pieces and live a normal life. And again, without any hard proof, that leaves all of those poor girls with no way to escape."

"I don't..."

Mackenzie stopped herself short before the entire comment came out of her mouth. She'd nearly said *I don't understand*. But the hell of it was, she thought she did. These women were terrified. They'd been brought up in terror, had it drilled into them, and then were abused as a reinforcement of that terror. Of course they were afraid to go public. It was yet another tactic it seemed Marshall Cole had carefully planted in place.

These women were already risking so much just being here, meeting with one another with her in tow. As an agent, it was beyond frustrating to see their pain yet not have them helping as much as she would like. But as a woman and a mother, she fully understood it.

Still, it did not make the fact that she would be heading back to DC tomorrow without closing the case any easier.

"I'm very sorry," Lilith said. "I have to go. If I'm not back in about an hour, someone might notice. And if Marshall arrives and he realizes I'm missing, he may ask more questions than usual."

"I understand," Mackenzie said. "But please, would you just think about it?"

Lilith only nodded as she fought back tears. She rolled up her window and quickly backed out of the parking spot.

Amy was also stifling back sobs as she started the car again. She looked earnestly over to Mackenzie. "I'm so sorry," she said.

"You have nothing to apologize for. If anything, I need to apologize to *you*. Maybe an agent worth a damn would have been able to find the killer without relying on the help of traumatized women."

"You did everything you could. But it's like I've been saying this entire time: the Community is untouchable."

Mackenzie had scoffed at the very notion of this yesterday. But now, as Amy pulled out and headed back toward Fellsburg, Mackenzie was starting to believe it herself.

Chapter Twenty Nine

Mackenzie was fine up until the moment she walked back into the Fellsburg PD. Something about the lights or the busyness of the place made her realize just how tired she was. She went back to the office she and Ellington had been using and found it empty. Amy tagged along behind her like a beaten puppy.

"Agent White? You think it would be okay if I went back to that holding cell? I'd really like some sleep."

Same here, girl, she thought.

"Sure. First, let's find Agent Ellington and Jane D—I mean, Ruth."

"You know...I really had no clue she was his daughter. And Lilith never told me, either. I guess she thought it would put more pressure on me to make sure she made it through alive."

"It's okay," Mackenzie said. "This whole thing is screwed."

They found Ellington and Ruth in the back of the building. Ruth was doing exactly what Amy wanted to do and what Mackenzie planned to do as soon as she could. She was sleeping on the same cot Amy had used last night. Ellington was sitting on a chair, speaking in quiet tones with Burke.

"Everything okay?" Mackenzie asked.

"Yeah," Ellington said. "But we may have some bad news."

"What's that?"

"The officer that took Cole back to the Community...we had him sort of wait things out. We asked him to stay parked at the end of that road and wait to see what happened. He called us twenty minutes ago. Marshall Cole just left the Community."

"Lilith..." Amy said.

"Who?" Burke asked.

"The First Wife," Mackenzie answered. "Amy can fill you in. Do we know where he's going?"

"Common sense would say he's coming back here for his so-called daughter," Ellington answered, hitching a thumb to the holding cell behind him.

"He's not wasting any time," Mackenzie said. She sighed deeply and looked at Amy. "You understand that if she is indeed his daughter, we can't keep her. We can file complaints with the state and try to get child protective services involved but that's going to take several days to get passed, if not weeks."

"So what do we do?"

Before anyone could answer, a panicked-looking officer came in through the single door that led to the holding cells. "Sheriff, just a heads-up: Marshall Cole just got here. He's got a lawyer with him and a folder with some papers."

Amy leaned against the bars of the holding cell, slapping at them. "Ruth...wake up. Come on, quickly."

Ruth roused a bit. When her sleepy eyes fell on the FBI agents, they went wide. She sat up and took a moment to get her bearings straight. "What is it?" she asked. "What's wrong?"

"Is he your father?" Amy asked.

"No! What?...I don't understand."

"Stop," Amy said. "No lies. If he's your father tell us *now.* He's here and he's going to take you back unless you say something to prevent it."

Ruth looked trapped. The sadness that slowly crept into her face told them everything they needed to know, confirming Lilith's side of the story.

"He is, isn't he?" Mackenzie asked.

Weeping, Ruth nodded. "Yes. But he doesn't even care. He has ten kids and only pays attention to the boys. The only time he..."

"What?" Ellington asked. "Tell us anything that might make him look bad and we can keep this up for a while. You can stay here and—"

"No. I can't."

"Why not?" Mackenzie asked, fishing for anything. "Tell us anything, and—"

"Chill, Mac," Ellington said.

"What?"

"Just...trust me. Lay off and come out into the hall to talk with me for a s—"

The door was opened again. This time, a man in a suit came in ahead of an indignant Marshall Cole. He surveyed the room as if he were looking at ants and trying to figure out which one he'd be stomping first.

Finally, his eyes settled on Ruth. A sneer crossed his face as he stormed toward the cell. "You have her locked up like some common criminal, I see! Get her out this moment."

"She's not locked in," Burke said. "In fact, she asked to go in there to rest."

"Yes," Ellington said. "She was so tired from all the running. And do you know why she was running, Mr. Cole?"

"Watch your words carefully, Agent."

"She was running from *you*," Amy said.

"Nonsense." He opened the cell door and stood aside to allow his daughter to come out. "Ruth, you can set this straight. Were you trying to run away from the Community?"

She didn't answer at first, and Mackenzie dared to hope the girl was coming around—that she might help nail this asshole after all. But after about five seconds, she shook her head. He then motioned for her to come out and she did as instructed.

"What's this?" Mackenzie asked, plucking the folder from the hands of the suited man.

"Proof of birth," the lawyer said.

"Ah, but I thought birthdays weren't celebrated at the community."

"Births are," Cole said. "But the tradition of observing birthdays is not. It is selfish and teaches entitlement."

Mackenzie looked the documents over. From what she could tell, they were legit. It seemed the birth had occurred on the Community grounds but Ruth was then taken to a doctor at three days old for a check-up of sorts. Sure enough, Marshall Cole was listed as father, but the mother was listed only as *Mother*.

"So she bears your child but gets no mention on the records?" Mackenzie asked. "Man, you just hate women, huh?"

"Keep it up," Cole said. "I beg you . . . go where you know you want to. By the way, shouldn't the two of you be on the way home?"

Mackenzie felt Ellington gently tugging at her pinky. She looked to him and saw him give the slightest shake of the head. There was a steely look in his eyes, like he might be hiding something. She fought every instinct in her to fight what was happening and to trust her partner and husband instead.

Amy, however, showed no such restraint.

"Sheriff, you can't let this happen! Ruth! Tell them! Tell them what goes on there!"

But Ruth's head was lowered in shame and fear. When her father placed his arm around her shoulder, she cringed but said nothing.

Then, surprising everyone in the room, Amy took a striding step toward Cole and pummeled his back with her fists. "You let her go, you son of a bitch!"

Burke pulled her away, giving Cole a deadly look. Cole wheeled around on both of them with violence in his stare. But then he seemed to remember where he was and that his lawyer was in his company.

"You'll be glad to know I am not pressing charges against you, Ms. Campbell."

"Against *me*?" Amy screamed, incredulous. "What for?"

"For attempting to kidnap my daughter."

"You're insane," Amy spat. "You're a fucking maniac and I hope I get to watch you die one day."

"Charming. I'm so glad my daughter won't have to be around such influences."

And with that, Cole, his lawyer, and Ruth left the holding cell area. The door clanged shut behind them and right away Amy turned to the FBI agents.

"How could you let that happen?" she roared.

Burke held up a finger, a motion that irritated Mackenzie. She looked to Ellington, who was watching Burke closely. Burke looked through the small glass window in the door for a moment before turning to them.

"We're good," he said.

"I'm sorry," Ellington said, taking Mackenzie's hands. "We just didn't have time to tell you. About three minutes before you came in, we finished setting Ruth up with a wire. It took some convincing, but she agreed. And I couldn't say anything in front of Amy because we were afraid Amy's reaction might make her change her mind. I almost called to tell you, but I figured we'd stand a better chance getting her to go along with it if we made it seem like not that big of a deal."

Mackenzie hated to feel out of the loop, but the small sense of victory that swept through her made it better.

"Wait," Amy said. "So Ruth is wearing a wire? What exactly does that mean?"

"It means that anything Cole says around her, we're going to hear it," Burke said. He was opening the door and quickly ushering them all out into the station. Near the middle of the hallway, there was a single officer standing with another door already opened. He was a tall and young-looking man who looked both excited and dutiful as Burke led them into the room.

"Agents, this is our communications specialist and sometimes-IT guy, Officer Stevens."

"We're already up and running," Stevens said. "They've been in the car for about fifteen seconds."

The room was built to be a large office, but the only furniture was a small standing desk in the back corner and a large conference-style table against the opposite wall. It was here that the communications systems was set up. It was rather simple, actually; a laptop, some sort of AV box Mackenzie was not familiar with, and a small receiver showing a series of digital numbers and waves indicating the pitch and tone of the audio.

Stevens went to the AV box and adjusted the volume. He set aside a pair of headphones he had apparently been wearing to get the set-up running.

When Cole's voice came to them, it was soft and almost apologetic. "...and I know there are things you may not understand about why we live our lives the way we do," he was saying. "We can talk about that, you know. If you want I can let you speak with Lilith. I know some of the other girls have found her helpful."

Amy let out a little gasp as she heard Cole mention the name of her insider. Mackenzie found it unsettling, too. It made her wonder just how much Cole knew about how Lilith was helping.

"I know it might be hard to hear," Mackenzie told Amy. "But even the slightest hint that he knows about the killings, and we not only find the killer, but we bring Marshall Cole down, too."

Amy nodded her understanding and leaned against the wall, listening. But other than the quiet and muffled sniffs and sobs from Ruth, there was no noise within the car. Mackenzie tried to imagine what it must be like within the car in that moment—Ruth, scared of her father and probably all kinds of paranoid because she was wearing the wire. And then there was Marshall Cole, thinking he had won.

"Amy, look . . . I think you being here is only going to make it more stressful on you," Ellington said. "Maybe you should go home and get some sleep."

"He's right," Mackenzie said. "But I swear, we'll keep you posted as soon as we hear anything."

She gave them both a perplexed look. "Are you crazy? You got Cole and you got Burton, but the killer was never caught. And he killed Shanda . . . and that means he knows where I live. There's no way I'm going back home until the killer has been caught."

Mackenzie wanted to argue against this and tell her they'd post an officer by her house. But she knew Amy had a point; she'd never be able to properly rest *anywhere*, let alone the house her friend had been killed in, until the killer was caught.

"That's fine, then," Burke said. "You're welcome to the cot in the holding cell."

Amy nodded to the audio equipment, still picking up nothing more than the hum of Cole's vehicle and the occasional sniffle from Ruth.

As they listened to the silence, a thought slowly occurred to Mackenzie. It was based on the brief exchange they'd just shared with Amy. They had known ever since Shanda's murder that neither Cole not Barton was the killer. However, whoever had been directing it all seemed to have known when and where the girls were meeting. She had assumed, after learning about Lilith, that someone must have been on to her.

But what if it was simpler than that? After all, it seemed the killer (or the one directing the killing) knew every detail—even where Amy lived.

Had they all been so absolutely blinded by their distaste for Marshall Cole that every single one of them had looked past what might be the most sensible answer?

What if Bob Burton had been sent to distract them? What if his appearance at the scene of Ruth's rescue had been a distraction so the real killer could make it to Amy's house to kill Shanda and, presumably, Amy if she had been there?

The silence was broken as Cole spoke up again. "You'll be okay," he said. "You'll see. Soon enough, you will be free of the doubts and fear that caused you to stray. We're almost home."

The comment was chilling. And it seemed to push Mackenzie's growing theory along a bit faster.

"Sheriff Burke, Officer Stevens, can you stay here with Amy?"

"Of course," Burke said. "Why? Where are you going?"

She looked to Ellington and said: "I know who the killer is. And if that comment Cole just made is any indication, I don't think we have much time."

"Then I guess we'd better haul ass then," Ellington said.

As they made their way out the door, Mackenzie heard one last comment from Cole come through the wire.

"And here we are, my love. Home sweet home, right?"

His daughter responded with a little moan that pushed Mackenzie straight out of the room.

CHAPTER THIRTY

Having shared her theory with Ellington while she sped north, she was certain she was right. Sometimes it took speaking something out to loud to understand just how much weight it carried. And although Ellington seemed skeptical at first, understanding dawned in his eyes as she neared the end of it.

"If you're right, that means..."

"It means I was blinded by an absolute hatred of Marshall Cole. And I think he planned on it. I think he's been using little set-ups like this ever since the Community started. He can hide behind his religious freedom, but deep down he's a master manipulator, too."

"I want to catch the killer as badly as you do," Ellington said. "But I have to admit, there's a little part of me that hopes you're wrong about this."

"Same here," she said.

But she knew she was right.

She sped north, sickened at how familiar the roads had become to her—having seen them on her way to the crash scene where Bethany and Felicia had died, taking Bob Barton into the police station, and their first visit to the Community. She hung a hard right, blasting by the BP station and getting the rental car up to eighty before having to slow it down for the next turn.

"I'd like to arrive there alive, if it's all the same to you," Ellington joked.

Mackenzie barely even gave him a smirk. Her eyes were glued to the road and every muscle in her body was tensing up for what was to come.

Up ahead, on the right, she saw the break along the trees where the gravel road that led to the Community started. She wondered how much time she'd managed to shave off by speeding here. She wondered how many minutes ahead of them Cole might have been. Fifteen? Surely no more than twenty.

She slowed and pulled onto the gravel. When she sped forward, she kicked up some gravel and the back end of the car started to slide to the left. At the same time, she heard her phone ringing. She dug it out and tossed it to Ellington so he could answer it.

"It's Burke."

"Speaker," she said. She knew she tended to get bossy when she was in the zone, but Ellington had told her long ago that it was one of the things he admired about her. He even joked that it was a huge benefit to him in the bedroom.

"This is Ellington," he answered.

"You guys almost there?"

"Maybe thirty seconds from the gate. You good on your end?"

"No. Things are getting bad over there. He's speaking in a way that gives us more and more evidence that *something* is going down, but nothing worthy of an arrest."

"Anything on the killings?"

"No. But Ruth is crying hysterically and I hear a lot of voices."

Mackenzie saw the place in the road where the gravel slowly faded out, leaving only the dirt track. She crested the slight rise along the road as Burke went on.

"Shit. Guys . . . this is bad. Ruth is screaming and there are . . . there are tons of other voices. They can't . . . *right there! Right there!* He just said he allowed the others to die. I barely heard it because of Ruth's screams. I'm sending backup for you."

"Thanks," Mackenzie said.

But honestly, she barely heard him. Ahead, she saw the fence and the gate. She saw a small moving shape in the little hut that had been unoccupied on the first visit.

Mackenzie stared the gate down as the car bumped along the dirt road. After clearing a bump, she pressed the gas down even further. The car lurched and Ellington looked over to her with a bit of concern in his eyes.

"What are you doing?" But he asked in a way that indicated he knew full well what she was doing.

"Right now, I'm really hoping the man at the security shack gets out of my way."

As the car rocketed toward the gate, she was relieved to see that the man *did* move. When the car was within twenty feet of the Community's front gate and showed no signs of slowing, the man dove out of a door in the back.

"Buckled in?" Mackenzie asked.

"No..."

"Then hold on to something."

Ellington braced himself against the dashboard with his hands as the car barreled forward. He closed his eyes slightly while Mackenzie bore down on the steering wheel braced for impact.

The gate gave way a little easier than she had been expecting. The dirt road had only allowed her to reach a speed of fifty before the car slammed into the gate. The section of fence that served as the gate buckled inward, tearing down a chunk of fence to the right as well. The posts that were bolted into the side of the little security shack pulled free, taking chunks of wood and plaster with it. Nearly half of the right side of the shack was torn free by the front of the car.

The sound inside the car was, Mackenzie was ashamed to say, rather delightful. The rattling of the chain-link fence and the shattering of wood and plaster from the hut was like music. She could literally feel her adrenaline spike as the gate tore free.

She hit the brakes and she looked through the windshield. Miraculously, the glass had suffered no damage. Through it, she could see a large crowd of people gathered off to the right, partially hidden by one of the smaller rows of small homes several yards away from the gate.

"You okay?" she asked Ellington.

"A little scared of you, but good to go."

Mackenzie opened the driver's side door carefully, looking for the man who had been stationed at the shack. She figured if he was serving as security there was a good chance he had some sort of firearm on him. But he was nowhere to be found.

She opened her door a bit wider as Ellington got out on the passenger's side. As she placed a foot on the ground, a gunshot rang out. She felt the shot land right in the middle of the door. She glanced to the right and saw the security guard tucked away behind a small mound of fill dirt along the back of what remained of the guard shack.

She drew her weapon to fire but Ellington beat her to it. He fired a well-placed shot that took the man just above the knee. He keeled over and when he did, Mackenzie and Ellington both raced over to him. As they did, Mackenzie looked back to the crowd of people down below. All of them were facing their way. There looked to be hundreds of them.

And some of them were coming their way. The man in front was holding a fragmented two-by-four.

Mackenzie kicked the guard's firearm away while Ellington searched him for more weapons. Taking out his handcuffs and applying them to the guard with expert ease, he looked back down to the crowd as well.

"You think they'll expect us to pay for the shack?" he asked.

Mackenzie saw that more of them were moving forward now. Beyond the two-by-four, she saw a hammer in the hand of another man.

"I think they'll expect us to pay for *something*," she said.

She brought her gun up just as Ellington fell in beside her. He did the same, both guns now aimed at the crowd, Mackenzie did her best to look beyond the approaching figures. She saw a broken circle of people behind them. There was a girl on the ground who looked to be crying. Her shoes and pants were in a heap off to the side. Her shirt had been torn, but still covered her.

When the girl looked slightly to the left, Mackenzie could see enough of her face to identify her.

It was Ruth. The Community must have been in the middle of some sort of sacrifice or punishment.

Mackenzie felt it was madness to do so, but she took two steps toward the approaching crowd. She didn't even bother trying to count. She guessed there were maybe fifty or sixty people moving toward them. At least two or three hundred were packed in behind them, all looking to see what would happen.

"We are federal agents," Mackenzie shouted. "Step any closer—especially those of you with weapons in your hands—and we will have no choice but to open fire."

A few of the approaching people hesitated for a moment, but the bulk of them continued to advance. Mackenzie took a few more steps forward, closing the distance between herself and the closest person in the crowd to about twelve feet. At her advancement, a few more stopped moving ahead but the majority of them were not swayed.

"When do we start shooting?" Ellington asked.

"I don't kn—"

"Everyone, stop!"

The voice came from further back, a loud and hoarse male voice. The crowd apparently knew the voice well because everyone in the approaching mob obeyed right away. The crowd started to part a bit in the back, allowing the speaker to come forward. Before the man reached the front of the crowd Mackenzie caught sight of the top of the man's head and knew that it was Marshall Cole.

"Everyone just stop right now! This is getting out of hand!"

Every person Cole passed by regarded him with a look of reverence. Some people looked as if they were actually afraid to look at him. And of course, the group that had been advancing on Mackenzie and Ellington were all men.

Cole saw the agents and actually smiled at them. It was a wide smile that did not fit the situation at all. His gate had been crashed and his security guard had been shot and handcuffed. Yet here Cole was, *smiling*.

"Tell me," he said with the smile on his face. "Did your hatred and misunderstanding for people you simply don't understand truly consume you so much that you felt this was in order?"

He gestured to the crashed gate and the car behind them. The car's hood was dented, both headlights were busted, and little wisps of gray steam came from under the hood.

"No, your crimes and abuse are what bought us back."

"Ah, I assume you think you have more evidence?"

"We do, as a matter of fact."

"I'd love to hear what it is. I think we'd *all* love to hear what it is."

She wanted to tell him very badly. But they apparently had not found Ruth's wire yet. Perhaps it had been hidden under her shirt. If it had been done to protocol, it was likely taped to her back.

As Cole mocked them, Mackenzie noticed that a few members of the group immediately behind him slowly started to break away to the right and left. She knew the maneuver right away; they were trying to very slowly and very subtly encircle them.

"Don't even think about it," she said. "No one move!"

"Or what, Agent White?" Cole said. "You seem to be a smart yet inherently stubborn woman. Think about your situation. You're alone, on private land.

There are two of you and nearly nine hundred of us. How many bullets do those guns carry when put together? Twenty-four? Thirty? Once you've expelled those, what do you think will happen to you?"

"Maybe the same thing you're doing to Ruth down there?"

"Oh, probably much worse. Ruth is simply being shown what happens to those that disobey. She'll be a good girl when it's all over."

Cole took a step forward, as did the other men all around and behind him. Mackenzie stood her ground, though she did step closer to Ellington. She had no delusions of leaving as a hero, guns blazing and making arrests left and right. She'd done what she'd set out to do; she'd stopped them from doing whatever they had planned to do to Ruth—for now at least.

For a fleeting moment, she saw a face in the back of the gathered crowd. Not a man, but a woman. And it brought her closer to the reason she had come speeding over here in the first place.

"Lilith," Mackenzie said. She didn't shout it, but her voice had a booming quality to it.

Cole smiled again. "Ah, so you know my wife? The Elder Wife, as it were." He looked back through the crowd and made a beckoning motion. Slowly, Lilith made her way through the crowd as they parted the same way they'd done for Cole.

When Lilith reached the front of the crowd, she made no attempt to play the part she had performed so well for Amy. She lovingly wrapped her hands around Cole's arms and regarded the scene with concern and victory in her eyes.

And in that moment, Mackenzie knew the Community would not let them leave.

"Why'd you do it?" Mackenzie asked.

"Smart young lady," Lilith said. "Not unlike so many of the women here in the Community. I think Marshall just now told you why I did it. Young ladies that step out of line or speak ill of our life and our ways must be punished."

"Killed?"

"In extreme cases, yes."

"So it was you?"

Lilith frowned and nodded her head slowly. "I had to do it. As the Elder Wife, it was my responsibility to see to it that the women that were not compliant were dealt with. Of course, I was not the only one. I led it all, yes. But many of us have killed as of late. It is our duty to keep the Community in a state of agreement."

That, at least, explained why Bob Barton had showed up at the BP station. He had indeed intended to kill the latest escapee with his crowbar, under Lilith's directions.

"Murder," Ellington said. "That seems like something your husband would be better suited for."

"Or was he too busy raping young women and arranging sham marriages?" Mackenzie asked.

"Back to the insults, I see," Cole said. "In the end, it always comes down to that." He sighed, as if he were very bored. "Would you like to come watch? Yes, I think you should see what we must do to Ruth. She's back home, which is the most important thing, of course. But you're just in time to see her punishment. It's something I think you, Agent White, could learn from."

Cole gestured for a few of the nearby men to take Mackenzie and Ellington. The one closest to them went for Ellington first. He was not violent at all; he simple walked to Ellington as if ready to escort him down an aisle.

When the man got too close, Ellington decked him with a quick right hand. The man dropped like a sack of rocks. The man who then came for Mackenzie caught a similar fate as she brought her knee up into the fork of his legs. He dropped down next to the other man. Behind them, at least ten more were angling forward.

"I *will* open fire!"

"I don't doubt it," Cole said. "Do that, though, and we will kill Ruth. And her blood will be on your hands. It will be your fault."

The rage inside of her was like poison. The mere idea of giving in to him made her sick. But she knew backup was on the way. And if she gave him this little bit of satisfaction, it would buy them some time. She just hoped Burke and his men got here before anything too bad could happen to Ruth.

"Fine," she said. Ellington, apparently on the same mental wavelength, gave a grunt and a nod as he holstered his sidearm.

"I think not," Cole said. "Drop the guns on the ground and put your hands on your head."

Feeling that it could be potentially dangerous, Mackenzie did as he asked. Ellington did the same and they both placed their hands on their heads.

Nearly right away, the man with the two-by-four came charging forward. He struck Ellington in the stomach with it, causing the board to crack even further. Ellington gasped and went to one knee. He then looked up to Cole with more anger than Mackenzie had ever seen in his eyes. It was unnerving; she was pretty sure Ellington would happily strangle Cole with his bare hands if given the chance.

"Enough of that," Cole said. He looked to the two men beside him and smiled. "Grab them and bring them down."

When the man on the right pushed Mackenzie forward, he went out of his way to make sure his right hand grabbed her breast. She had to clasp her hands on top of her head to make sure she didn't attack the asshole.

They led Mackenzie and Ellington down to where the larger crowd was gathered. The crowd parted to let them through, as if they were cherished guests.

When Mackenzie saw Ruth on the ground, she nearly screamed and turned to fight until the death. She just didn't care anymore.

No, she thought. *Don't be stupid. Backup is coming. Just hang in there a few more minutes . . .*

She could do that. She *had* to do that.

But then she saw the twelve men holding the bats and iron rods and all of that changed.

CHAPTER THIRTY ONE

Ruth saw them and moaned something to them. Mackenzie could see where Ruth had recently been struck in the face. Her bottom lip was busted open and there was a perfect imprint of an open hand on her right cheek. Her pants and underwear had been removed. Mackenzie wasn't one hundred percent sure, but she thought she saw a bite mark on the young woman's right buttock.

"Please," Ruth said. "Help..."

All around them, the crowd that had been advancing toward Mackenzie and Ellington just moments ago fell into the circle. The number of people was dizzying. The size of the circle was large enough to fit a modest house in, but it only contained Ruth. She was kneeling on the grass, her hands and ankles tied.

The twelve men with the belts and little iron whips stepped forward into the clearing with Ruth. Mackenzie eyed the little rods; they looked almost like the antennas from old-school radios. These twelve made another circle around her, an inner circle of sorts. When this was formed, Lilith entered the circle. She reached Ruth, bowed to Cole, and then he also entered the circle.

Mackenzie hated to do it, but she looked away from Ruth. She had to find some way to stop this. She looked everywhere but saw no solution. She angled her head back, trying to find out who had their weapons. She then spotted the man that she'd kneed in the crotch and saw that he had both of them. In her mind, she placed an imaginary target on him.

They had kept Mackenzie and Ellington together. She assumed the plan was for them to suffer whatever fate was about to be doled out to Ruth.

She looked back to the circle and saw the ritual was still being played out. Cole looked to a man at the outer rim of the circle and gave him a nod. "Take your places," Cole said.

155

At this command, the men with whips and belts took a few steps away from one another. At their feet, Ruth screamed. Behind her, a line started to form, breaking away from the circle. They were all men, aged anywhere between eighteen and sixty or so. The one in front led the line up next to the men with weapons. It was not clear what was going on, but Mackenzie made an assumption that disgusted her: a woman, stripped of her pants and underwear, tied up with a line of men behind her.

"E, I can't...I can't let it happen..."

Cole stood by Ruth. He reached down and caressed the side of her face. She screamed in response. Cole then hooked his fingers in the collar of her shirt and pulled it roughly over her head. The point, Mackenzie assumed, was to degrade her by showing more skin.

They had not expected to see the little black pack taped to her back, though.

"What is this?" Cole asked, genuinely confused and surprised. He looked to Ruth and then to Mackenzie and Ellington.

When he locked eyes with Mackenzie, she gave him a grin. "That," she said, "is our new evidence, you son of a bitch."

Cole reached down and tore the pack off. The tape came away violently, causing Ruth to scream. Cole threw the AV pack on the ground and then pointed at Mackenzie and Ellington.

"You watch now! You! You have caused this." He then turned to the men with the belts and gave them a nod. "Now. Skip the formalities and do it *now!*"

Two of the men raised their belts over their shoulders.

Mackenzie acted on pure adrenaline and instinct. In that moment, she did not care what became of her. She could not stand by and allow this to happen. She moved so quickly that the man holding her had no chance of stopping her.

She dashed forward. Some poor soul beside her stepped out to stop her but she threw out her right elbow as if it were on a mechanical release and downed the man easily. She barreled forward and, unsurprisingly, Cole moved out of the way. She dove for the two men who had raised their belts, knowing she could not take them both out. Still, she did her best.

Just before her shoulders collided with the knees of the man on the right, there was a loud *crack* as the belt came down. It slapped her right across the back and though her shirt softened the blow, the pain was immense. She did not cry out, though. Instead, she funneled that pain towards her anger and got to her feet right away.

She saw that several people were coming for her and that Ellington was engaged in a fight of his own. She barely caught sight of another of the men with a belt. He raised it up, aiming it for her face. When it came down, Mackenzie braced herself for the pain as she brought her arm up to block it. Not only was she able to block it, she managed to wrap her hand around the belt. She gave a tug, and though the belt did not come free of the man's hands, it did bring him forward. He tumbled toward her and she met him with a punch to the face. As he staggered back, she pulled the belt free.

She wasted no time, wheeling around and slapping the person closest to her. She caught the man on the arm. Someone caught her from behind, placing an arm around her neck. She arched her back, grabbed the arm, and tossed them over her shoulder. They went sailing into three other people and it was in seeing *that* that made Mackenzie realize how much trouble they were really in.

But that's when the first gunshot rang out. A man screamed and for a moment, she was sure it was Ellington. But when she looked for the source of the shot, she saw an older man staggering backward with blood coming out of his shoulder. Below him, on the ground, Ellington was getting to his feet with one of their guns. The other, she saw, was on the ground at his feet. One of Cole's men dove for it, but Ellington kicked him in the face for his efforts.

Another man came running for Ellington, screaming in terror. Mackenzie was helpless but to watch as Ellington shot the man. The round went into the man's stomach. He took one more step forward before he collapsed.

In front of her, Cole was screaming for people to attack, to get the agents, to kill them.

But his voice was soon overtaken by the sounds of sirens. Several people heard it all at once, looking back toward the direction of the ruined gate. Mackenzie took advantage of the momentary distraction to angle herself back over toward Ellington.

Cole did his best to regain composure. He still stood by Ruth, regarding the panicking crowd. "Everyone, as you were! Calm down! We've done nothing wrong here!"

Mackenzie couldn't help herself. As Cole went on with his little diatribe, she gripped the belt and flicked it forward like a bullwhip. The crack it made in the air was buried under the commotion of the crowd, but she *saw* the effects. It caught Cole right in the mouth. He stumbled backward, his hand flying to his face. She wanted to do it again and again, but ran to Ellington's side.

As he handed her the other gun, a brave soul ran up to both of them and spit in Ellington's face. Mackenzie delivered a stiff right hand that caught the man in the throat. Two more men were coming at them, one of whom Mackenzie took out with a shot to the lower leg. This made the other one back up and with that, most everyone within the Community decided the time for the attack was over.

The sirens had reached them now as two police cars pulled in through the crashed front gate. And as Mackenzie looked in that direction, watching Sheriff Burke get out of his car, she saw a third and a fourth pulling behind them as well.

Then, as she and Ellington stood back to back, keeping an eye out for any remaining brave and foolish would-be attackers, she heard the unmistakable stuttering noise of an approaching helicopter. She looked up and to the left, where a small speck approaching form the north got gradually closer.

Then, realizing that no one else was going to come for them—most of them were running in a panic, some into their homes and others toward the gate as they tried to escape the Community—Mackenzie dashed down to where Ruth was still on the ground. The girl tensed up a bit when Mackenzie gently took her shoulders.

"Ruth, it's okay. It's me . . . you're okay now."

Mackenzie started undoing the ropes around Ruth's wrists as the girl began to cry uncontrollably. A few people eyed them as they went rushing past, but Mackenzie ignored them. She sat there, holding Ruth against her, as Burke and his men stormed the grounds and the helicopter started to slowly land just outside the Community's fence.

CHAPTER THIRTY TWO

Following the ordeal on the Community grounds, Burke insisted that Mackenzie and Ellington get some sleep. He even volunteered to put them up in Fellsburg's only motel. And while the prospect of sleep seemed glorious (she'd had only a twenty-minute nap in the last forty-two hours), Mackenzie refused.

The police presence within the Community grounds remained there for nearly twenty-four hours after the helicopter touched down. During the day or so that followed, Mackenzie and Ellington did indeed catch some sleep, but only in little sporadic power naps here and there.

Within the first hour, the Salt Lake City FBI had also arrived on the scene. State police reinforcement had also showed up. Hundreds of Community residents did their best to escape but most were stopped by law enforcement. This resulted in quite a few brawls, some of which nearly got so out of hand that there was a conversation about calling in reinforcements from the National Guard.

In the end, such measures weren't needed. By seven o'clock that evening, there were more than one hundred and twenty law enforcement personnel on the grounds. The Community members were filed into different sectors, quickly interrogated, and, in most cases arrested or charged. Those that were not charged but had nowhere to go were housed in temporary tents that the State Police set up several yards outside of the Community grounds. When it was quite clear that many of the women were traumatized and had been abused, counselors and other mental health professionals were called to the site.

As ten o'clock rolled around, Mackenzie found herself sitting in the passenger's seat of the car she had wrecked through the gate. In the busyness of the day, it had been pulled away from the gate and set to the side. Mackenzie sat in the seat and watched the lines of Community residents as they were led through makeshift kiosks the State Police had set up in the field in front of the fences. There were so many people and so much going on that Mackenzie still wasn't sure how it was working. She supposed, aside from the idiots who had tried to escape, a great deal of the Community residents may even be glad this had happened. Perhaps the level of violence and chaos wasn't so bad because many of them *wanted* a different life.

She spotted a figure walking over toward her. The shape was mostly shadow, cast and stretched by the multiple floodlights that had been set up around the grounds. As the figure drew closer to the car, Mackenzie saw that it was Amy. The young woman came over to the driver's side and knocked on the door.

"Come on in," Mackenzie said.

Amy opened the door and slid into the driver's seat. "I understand you used this as a battering ram earlier today."

"Yeah. It's just hard for me to think of it as *today*. Seems like forever ago."

"You okay?"

"Yeah. I'm exhausted, though."

"Where's your partner?"

"He's out there somewhere. He thrives under this sort of stuff. He hasn't had any sleep either but he's on cloud nine right now."

"Agent White, I wanted to thank you. You tried so hard to get me to reveal things and I was stubborn. I could have made this a lot easier ..."

"It's okay. You were scared. I get it. I *especially* get it after seeing what they were about to do to Ruth today. I had no idea it was that bad. Honestly, I respect the hell out of you for trying to help those girls."

"They were going to punish her, weren't they? In front of the entire community?"

"Yeah."

"I sometimes wonder what they would have done to me if they'd captured me back when I escaped. It would have been embarrassing for them, you know? To have to admit someone escaped. I think that's why Lilith killed those girls. To make sure no one ever knew. And you know what? I apologize for that, too."

"For what?"

"Being so blinded by it all and assuming Lilith was truly on my side. You saw through it in just a few days and I ... I would have never seen it."

"Amy, stop that. Your life has been a mess because of these people and you're just going to allow them to have more power over you. Besides, I think it's safe to say *you* were the one who gave those girls hope. You were the one who proved that it was possible to leave."

"And look what it got them," Amy said, starting to cry. "I just wish...I wish she'd come for me. I wish she'd killed me and that would have been the end of it."

"You know why she didn't, right?"

Amy shook her head.

"She didn't kill you because you'd been gone for so long. If anyone at the Community ever happened to find out what was going on, they'd know you had escaped and stayed in hiding for so long. They were more interested in showing their power and control immediately—for girls that had *just* escaped. To kill you would mean having to face their failures."

Another thing she had thought of, but did not say in front of Amy, was that Lilith had likely planned the entire thing. In the same way Marshall Cole had so many loopholes and scenarios to make himself look stronger, Lilith had also devised a way to make sure she was able to keep the women in line: help them escape and then kill them right away.

"You have somewhere to go after all of this?" Mackenzie asked.

"I met with a counselor a few hours ago. She said she thinks it's a bad idea to go back to the house I was living in. She's working out how me and a few of the women can find some sort of state-funded housing to live together until we can get back on our feet."

"That's good," Mackenzie said. She wanted to say something else but, really, what else was there to say? *I'm sorry* didn't seem to cover the gamut of betrayal and pain Amy was currently experiencing.

"Anyway," Amy said. "I just wanted to apologize. You were trying to catch a nap, weren't you?"

"It's okay. I'll get some sleep soon enough."

Amy nodded and slowly got out of the car. Mackenzie watched the girl walk back over toward the tents. She looked in the direction of the Community, separated from her by only the chain-link fence. She stared in that direction for a while, as if trying to make sense of something. It broke Mackenzie's heart to see her standing like that, frozen between her horrific past and her future. Mackenzie kept her eyes on Amy until she stepped into one of the tents.

Then, with a faint smile on her face, Mackenzie drifted off to sleep.

She woke up some time later with Ellington lightly shaking her. She sat up with a gasp. She hadn't even realized she'd fallen asleep. She glanced to the digital clock in the dashboard and saw that somehow, it had gotten to be 2:15 in the morning.

"I hated to wake you up," Ellington said. "But I think you and I are done here for now. And I'd really like to take Burke up on that offer of a hotel room."

"You can drive," she said, already trying to recapture her sleep.

"Not this car," he said. "You sort of broke it."

She sighed and got out of the car with him. As she expected, she came more and more awake as she walked with him.

"Sorry I conked out on you."

"It's okay. You deserve it."

"So do you. But you weren't sleeping."

"That's because I have far more endurance than you," he joked.

He wrapped his arm around her and drew her close as they walked across the field. She saw that all of the tents were still standing. The lines looked shorter but the people manning those tents weren't going to be done anytime soon. The spotlights were also still up, shining down on the field and a currently empty Community.

"I don't think McGrath is going to like us staying in Utah one more day just so we can sleep."

"I already talked to him," Ellington said. "He approved it. The amount of information that is coming in about what's going on here has him a little flummoxed. He has complaints regarding us but stories of multiple arrests and saved women. It should be a very interesting meeting when we get back."

"Can you imagine writing up a report about this?"

"Not right now. And I don't even want to think about it until I get at least ten hours of sleep."

Mackenzie agreed. Ellington led her over to a Fellsburg patrol car. An officer Mackenzie had not yet met nodded to them and opened the back door for them. As Mackenzie got inside, she took one last look to the Community grounds. She was glad she was so tired and unable to fully comprehend the years and years of suffering and abuse that had taken place there. While she was glad to have helped bring it to an end, it did little to heal her heart toward women like Amy and Ruth. She couldn't imagine the things they had endured.

Softly, she cried into Ellington's shoulder. She closed her eyes and felt the bumps of the dirt road as the policeman took them away from the Community. Even through her closed eyes she could detect the glare of the spotlights but as soon as that glare faded, there was only the dark. And Mackenzie slipped into sleep again.

CHAPTER THIRTY THREE

One thing Director McGrath hated more than anything was for his agents to be involved in news coverage. Mackenzie supposed that was why he was in such a pissy mood when she and Ellington sat down in front of his desk. They'd left Utah, slept the sleep of the dead during the four-and-a-half-hour flight, and had come straight to his office. It had all occurred in a whirlwind and as she sat across from him, Mackenzie felt well-worn and exhausted. Four and a half hours on a plane was nothing, even after the day they had spent sleeping and working on their case report in the motel in Fellsburg.

McGrath looked across the desk at them, as he had many times before. He wasn't mad or upset exactly, but it was clear that something was troubling him. She saw a thin stack of papers on his desk and assumed it was the report she and Ellington had worked on yesterday in the motel.

Footage of the Community grounds was all over the news. She and Ellington had left the scene long before the media arrived, but their names were being mentioned in news reports. From what Mackenzie could gather, some of the women gave the reporters their names—probably Amy or Ruth, unaware of how difficult it might make things for them.

McGrath was likely aware of the reports. And that was probably the result of his odd and nearly bipolar mood. When he looked at both of them, though, she thought she saw something like amusement in his eyes. She couldn't be sure; it wasn't the sort of thing she was used to seeing out of him.

"You two," McGrath said, "are an absolute pain in my ass."

He let the comment linger for a moment. He looked down to the report and then back to them. He reclined back in his seat and shook his head.

"I got a call twenty minutes ago," he said. "It was from the director of the Salt Lake City branch. The numbers aren't finalized yet, but here's what we have so far. Four hundred and eleven arrests. *Four hundred. And. Eleven.* And the two of you opened the door for that. Four hundred and eleven arrests, all of men who were abusing the women in the Community. Marshall Cole is, of course, among that number. His trial should be interesting... but I digress. Out of that entire scene at the Community two days ago, there were zero deaths. Not a single one. There were several injuries, however. And that's where this conversation is going to turn a little bleak."

Mackenzie thought of the crowd falling in on her, of knowing full well they would have to fire their guns to fend the Community members off. She also recalled the mad dash as many of those same members had attempted to escape.

"Any idea how many members are unaccounted for?" Mackenzie asked.

"It's harder for them to tell that sort of thing for sure, but they're estimating somewhere around one hundred."

"And the women?" Ellington asked.

"It's still being sorted out. Most of them were over eighteen so Child Protective Services isn't being absolutely flooded. It does create a nightmare for the state as they try to find medical and mental help. And housing... but you can get that information later. For now, we need to go over the formalities of it all."

"Formalities?" Ellington asked.

"Yeah. Amid all of these amazing numbers for arrests and lives saved that are coming, there are complaints, too. Most are from the Community members that are being placed under arrest. I've got reports that indicate the following." He stopped here to pick up a piece of paper sitting off to the side of their case report. "Driving a car through a gate and trespassing on private property. Shooting a security guard. Shooting at least three other Community members. Physical assault, including Marshall Cole being whipped across the face with a belt. There are more here, but they are minor."

"That sounds bad," Mackenzie said, "but you saw the report. If we didn't get in there, God only knows what they would have done to Ruth Cole."

"Oh, I'm aware. Her testimony is one of the darkest, most gruesome things I've ever heard. Still, despite the heroism the two of your displayed, there are certain measures and rules we have to follow."

Mackenzie had been expecting this, so she wasn't too upset or depressed.

"The security guard fired first from what I understand," McGrath said. "So I can swipe that one away...even though he fired at you as a result of you crashing a car into his gate." He stopped here and Mackenzie could hardly believe her eyes when it looked as if he were actually grinning. "But the ones you shot during the...the *fallout*. You yourself said in your reports that those people were mostly unarmed. And it's *those* cases we have to look at."

"Director, we had no choice..." Ellington said.

"I know. And I've already spoken to members of the committee that decide what sort of punishments come out of scenarios like these. You'll be pleased to know that everyone up the ladder, all the way to the top, are thrilled about this outcome. No one on our side of the line thinks anything you did was unforgiveable. If I'm being honest, seeing those women on television talking about how wonderful the two FBI agents were...it looks good for us. That's the plain and simple truth."

"But?" Mackenzie said.

"But there *are* complaints. And some of them are legitimate. So I have to do my job and dole out punishment."

Ellington sighed, but Mackenzie simply sat there, ready to accept whatever came.

"The committee and myself decided that we had to do *something*. Now, we've made it look much worse on paper, but your disciplinary action comes down to a three-week suspension for both of you, with pay."

They both waited for him to keep going. When he did not, Mackenzie quietly asked: "That's it?"

"That's it. Three weeks. Take it. Sleep. If you don't mind my saying, you both still look like death warmed over."

"Thanks, sir."

McGrath smiled. While it still looked odd on him, it warmed Mackenzie's heart a bit. He was not the same man she'd first met a little over four years ago. She liked to think she'd had a little something to do with that.

"Anything else, sir?" Mackenzie asked, getting to her feet.

"Yes." He rubbed at his head and sighed. "We're already getting calls from news outlets and publishers, wanting to speak with you. Should they end up contacting you during your suspension, do the bureau a favor and ignore them." He waved them away and turned his attention to the report on his desk.

When they were back out in the hallway of the bureau headquarters, Mackenzie reached over and took Ellington's hand. "Funny," she said. "He called it a suspension, but why did I hear *vacation*?"

"Vacation?" he asked. "Unless you have forgotten, we still have mother drama waiting for us back at home."

"Oh yeah. Damn."

He squeezed her hand as they came to the elevators. They stepped on and as the doors slid closed in front of them, he pulled her close and kissed her deeply as if to make her forget all about it.

When they arrived back at their apartment, the surprises continued. As soon as Ellington unlocked the door and announced himself, Mackenzie could smell something cooking. Bacon, maybe, or some other kind of breakfast meat. Her stomach reminded her how ravenous she was (the airline meal had done absolutely nothing for her).

She was about to ask what smelled so good when she saw her mother.

She was sitting at the table in the dining area. There was a sandwich in front of her, currently uneaten; her attention was on Kevin, who was currently at work on a banana. Elsewhere, the vacuum cleaner was running.

"Mom," Mackenzie said. "What are you doing here?"

She shrugged. "Swallowing my pride, I suppose."

"I thought you were flying home?"

Ellington, meanwhile, took a moment to swing by the highchair to kiss Kevin on the head. Kevin grinned and offered his banana. Ellington took a bite, which amused Kevin. He cackled and then frowned as Ellington made a quick exit in search of the vacuum cleaning noise—and to give Mackenzie and her mother some time alone.

"Yes, I *was* going to fly home. But then Frances called me. At the time, I thought she was being rather rude. She's a sweetheart, really, but she doesn't have much of a filter."

"Oh yes, I know."

Mackenzie took the other seat by Kevin. Seeing his mother so close, he tossed the banana down and flexed his little hands, asking to be picked up.

Mackenzie used his bib to wipe his hands and took him out of the seat. She gave him a hug while he tried to brace his little legs on her knees.

"Anyway," Patricia went on. "She told me that I was being selfish. She told me I was not thinking of you or of Kevin. At first, I exploded on her and used lots of colorful words. She gave some right back and, oddly enough, that's what it took. We talked it out. I pulled over on the side of the highway and we talked it out. I came back..."

"You didn't answer any of my calls."

"I know. I should have, and I'm sorry. But I wasn't in any position to talk to you so soon after having it out with Patricia."

The sound of the vacuum cleaner came to a stop. She could hear Ellington and his mother speaking softly in the living room.

"I'm sorry if I was hard on you for calling," Mackenzie said. "But this case was—"

"Oh, I know all about the case. It's been all over the news."

"Yeah," chimed Patricia, entering the kitchen with Ellington behind her. He gave Mackenzie an *is-this-okay* look and she nodded. "Both of your names have been all over the news. Your phones haven't been blowing up?"

"Not exactly," Ellington said.

"Anyway," Patricia continued, "Frances helped me realize that even though we're vastly different in our parenting styles, there is one thing we have in common."

"I can't even imagine what that might be," Mackenzie said, being quite serious.

"Broken relationships with our children."

"That's right," Frances said. "We've been sharing horror stories about you two for the last two days."

"Oh my God," Ellington said.

"Quiet, you," Mackenzie said. "I'd personally love to hear horror stories about E as a child."

"Grab a drink, then," Patricia said with a laugh. "We're going to be a while!"

Ellington picked up Kevin and dramatically stormed out of the kitchen. "I hate you all," he called out over his shoulder.

The three women sitting at the table shared a laugh and for just a moment, Mackenzie forgot how tired she was.

❧   ❧   ❧

She got a bit more sleep that afternoon, napping when Kevin took his afternoon nap. When she woke up, she finally felt like she might have caught up on her sleep—eleven hours in the Fellsburg motel, four hours on the flight home, and an hour and a half after sitting around the dining room table speaking with both grandmothers.

When she came out of the bedroom, she saw her mother rolling her suitcase to the front door. They'd only briefly spoken about when she would leave but had not decided on anything before her nap.

"I guess you're leaving this afternoon?" Mackenzie said.

"Yeah. With both of you back home, I don't see the point in hanging around. I don't want to be in the way."

"You have to stop thinking like that, Mom. You won't be in the way. I promise. Stay. One more night."

"You sure?"

"Yeah. In fact, let me talk to E. Maybe him and his mom would be willing to stay here with Kevin while you and I go out for coffee or something."

"Now?"

Mackenzie had the foul taste of an afternoon nap in her mouth. She shook her head and said, "Give me ten minutes."

She brushed her teeth, got the naptime kinks out of her hair, and kissed Kevin goodbye. As she'd expected, Ellington had been absolutely fine with her stepping out for a bit. So, for the first time in their lives, Mackenzie and her mother intentionally went out together for no other reason than sharing time.

They settled on a Starbucks three blocks away from the apartment. It was getting close to dinnertime, so it wasn't too crowded. After ordering their drinks, they found a table near the back.

"So you're famous now, huh?" Patricia asked her daughter.

"Hardly. I was so-called famous before this. A case known as the Scarecrow Killer. It's how I became an agent, actually."

"Seems like something I should know. You know . . . being your mother and all."

"It's okay, Mom. You . . . yeah, you weren't perfect. I don't think any mother is. And you were absent, sure. But . . ."

"What?"

This case we just got back from. The things I saw ... I don't know. It made me appreciate what I have here. My life was not ideal growing up, but it could have been a hell of a lot worse."

"You need to talk about what happened out there?"

"Eventually. Not now, though. Right now, I can't even begin to process it."

Patricia looked awkward as she sipped her coffee and eyed her daughter. "I wish I knew what to do ... how to be there for you."

Mackenzie shook her head. "Mom, you need to understand something. I am beyond thrilled to have you back in my life. I really am. And the idea of you spending more and more time with Kevin makes my heart very happy. But I'm not expecting you to swoop in and make up for all of those lost years. Even if you'd been the best mother on the planet, there are just some things you can't be there for. That's what Ellington is here for." She meant it as a serious statement, but it brought a smile to her mother's face.

"I love that you call him by his last name."

"It's the bureau in me."

"Speaking of which ... picturing you in the midst of everything I saw on television about that awful cult made me realize how much of a ... I don't know ... a badass you are. I'm very proud of you."

"Thanks, Mom."

"And it was the terrible events around your father that got you here? To this career?"

"Yes. In a roundabout way."

"Have you ever talked to your sister about it?"

Mackenzie hid her response by taking a sip of her coffee.

"You reached out to me and we're here. Maybe if you reached out to her as well, that could be repaired."

"Maybe. And in time, I think I will. And you?"

"I keep trying, but she's not interested."

They thought about this for a moment, but it did not bother Mackenzie all that much. After what she'd seen and experienced in Fellsburg and now, having this surreal moment with her mother, Mackenzie thought maybe, at the heart of it, all things were possible.

"So on to the other things," Patricia said.

"Yes. Please."

"How many grandbabies do I get?"

Mackenzie nearly spit her coffee out. "You know," she said, joking, "somehow, I found it pretty easy to be apart from you."

They both laughed at this. And in that moment, the past collided with the future, molding itself into something other than an obstacle.

Epilogue

In the dream, it was not Ruth Cole that was bound with her backside exposed. Instead, it was her. It was Mackenzie. And in the circle of men with belts and iron rods, she saw her father and Ellington. She saw the man she had once, long ago, known as the Scarecrow Killer. And Marshall Cole was there, too. He was grinning, his lip busted from the belt.

Lilith stood beside him. She was naked, taking on the pose of Eve in just about every Renaissance painting there was. The women of the Community rallied behind her. They were well-groomed and beautiful, watching events unfold.

In the dream, there was no one there to help. The fate she had spared Ruth from was dished out on her.

She'd wake up screaming and flinch at Ellington's touch. Eventually she would nestle into him, sweating and weeping from the dream. She would feel sleep pulling at her but did not want to go back, in the event the dream was still there, waiting for her.

Exactly thirty-nine days after Mackenzie White had crashed her car through the gate of a religious compound known as the Community, she got an email that filled her with more emotion than she thought she was capable of.

Her three-week suspension was over, but because the media was still looking for any tidbits on what had gone down outside of Fellsburg, Utah, McGrath was having her and Ellington keep a low profile. She appreciated it because those three weeks had allowed her to heal, seeking out a therapist outside of the bureau and to truly work on herself.

She was sitting at her desk at work when the email came through. She did not recognize the email address, but the subject line was intriguing.

Thanks from the girls

Mackenzie opened it and nearly started weeping right away.

Agent White,

So, it's very hard to get the email address of one particular federal agent. Did you know that? I tied digging around online but couldn't find it. So I asked Sheriff Burke for it and he was able to get it for me. Not sure how, and I didn't ask.

I'm not exactly used to writing this sort of thing or using a computer for that matter. So Amy is doing her best to coach me through it. Please bear with me.

I'm writing this on a borrowed MacBook. I'm at a desk, looking out of a window and looking at the pretty spectacular view that is St. George, Utah. I had my final check-up today to make sure I had no infections or diseases from living at the Community for so long and I was finally given a clean bill of health. (I did have a case of something I'd rather not admit to, but it's all cleared up now.)

Amy told me to write you. I haven't really spoken to anyone about what happened to me. I'm seeing a therapist but haven't really opened up yet. I think it's coming, though. And here I go, rambling...

I wanted to thank you. It wasn't just that you got to the bottom of what was going on in the Community. It was that you came rushing in when they were about to start beating me. You did it fearlessly and with bravery like I've never seen. I'm going to take a leap here and assume you're a mother. Bunches of kids, I bet. Because that was some Momma Bear stuff you pulled out there to save me.

I'm living with two other girls from the Community in a pretty decent apartment. The state is covering us for now, and we have a career trainer coming in a few days to help us get established. We're working with state case workers, therapists, and a few Salt Lake City agents to help get to the nitty-gritty of what all went on there. Last I heard, Marshall is going to trial in about two weeks and he's going to get buried. As for Lilith, she managed to kill herself in her holding cell. Slit her wrists on the corner of her bed frame and bled out before they could save her.

I don't expect you to respond to this email. I know you must be busy with other cases and interviews and everything. But please know that I'm never going to forget what you did that day. Yes, you and your partner saved so many women from torture and abuse. But me, personally... I can't thank you enough. No one has ever stood up for me like that.

Now . . . if you don't have bunches and bunches of babies, I think you should. I don't really even know what it's like to have a mother, but if I did, I'd want her to be like you. Thank you, Agent White. I hope this email finds you well.

Kind Regards,
Ruth

Mackenzie smiled as she opened up the Reply tab. She wiped tears away and thought about Ruth from that day at the Community. To know that she was now getting on her feet and experiencing life in full for the first time was somehow beyond comprehension.

She did not think about her response very much at all. She just started writing, wanting it to be honest and unfiltered. And, most importantly, from the heart.

Ruth,

You guessed right. I am a mother. I have a handsome little man at home, creeping up on fourteen months. His name is Kevin and the poor kid is the spitting image of his father. Also (and no one knows this, not even the grandmothers, so shhh . . .) Agent Ellington and I have very recently started working on a second . . .

As she typed, Mackenzie thought of mothers and daughters. She thought of how no one's life ever truly turned out the way they wanted or expected. And while there was beauty in that, there was also a healthy amount of fear.

She tried to imagine the excitement and fear in Ruth Cole as she stared out of that apartment window, emailing someone on the other side of the country. She tried to imagine a girl who had never experienced the love of a mother or father and what a future of freedom might feel like—a girl staring out her window with such determination and perseverance that she almost *dared* the future to come to her.

It wasn't a bad place to be in. Mackenzie could easily remember making such a dare back before she'd become an agent. The future, of course, had taken her up on that dare, and it had brought her here, to this moment.

It wasn't ideal by any means, but as far as Mackenzie was concerned, it had all worked out.

Everything was perfect.

A New Series!

Now Available for Pre-Order!

LEFT TO DIE
(An Adele Sharp Mystery—Book One)

"When you think that life cannot get better, Blake Pierce comes up with another masterpiece of thriller and mystery! This book is full of twists and the end brings a surprising revelation. I strongly recommend this book to the permanent library of any reader that enjoys a very well written thriller."

—Books and Movie Reviews, Roberto Mattos (re Almost Gone)

LEFT TO DIE is book #1 in a new FBI thriller series by USA Today bestselling author Blake Pierce, whose #1 bestseller Once Gone (Book #1) (a free download) has received over 1,000 five star reviews.

FBI special agent Adele Sharp is a German-and-French raised American with triple citizenship—and an invaluable asset in bringing criminals to justice as they cross American and European borders.

When a serial killer case spanning three U.S. states goes cold, Adele returns to San Francisco and to the man she hopes to marry. But after a shocking twist, a new lead surfaces and Adele is dispatched to Paris, to lead an international manhunt.

Adele returns to the Europe of her childhood, where familiar Parisian streets, old friends from the DGSI and her estranged father reignite her dormant obsession with solving her own mother's murder. All the while she must hunt down the diabolical killer, must enter the dark canals of his psychotic mind to know where he will strike next—and save the next victim before it's too late.

An action-packed mystery series of international intrigue and riveting suspense, LEFT TO DIE will have you turning pages late into the night.

Books #2 and #3 in the series – LEFT TO RUN and LEFT TO HIDE – are also available for preorder!

LEFT TO DIE
(An Adele Sharp Mystery–Book One)

Did you know that I've written multiple novels in the mystery genre? If you haven't read all my series, click the image below to download a series starter!